WEB OF SECRETS

WEB OF SECRETS

DENISE HARRIS

PEEPAL TREE

First published in Great Britain in 1996
Peepal Tree Press Ltd
17 King's Avenue
Leeds LS6 1QS
England

© Denise Harris 1996

All rights reserved
No part of this publication may be
reproduced or transmitted in any form
without permission

ISBN 0 948833 87 4

In memory of
my mother

And for my Aunt Sheila

CHAPTER ONE

'... My opinion is that perhaps the whole thing started from that first ambush which happened so long ago that we have literally cast it aside... People ambushed against their wills, collared and brought by force to this country with only memories to carry them through... a place one would not put a name to from the very beginning, and even those memories had to be concealed and pressed down on for the sake of survival, but then those same memories would one day ambush us in return, as I see it, and don't take my word as gospel, but as I see it, Kathleen Harriot imagining she was seeing cracks was in fact ambushed by memories that were thought to be dead and buried and in fact were only lying low, so they resurfaced and then things started happening... it's a matter of psychology. I lived on the same street with the Harriots. When I saw what became of her I said to myself it's all a matter of psychology... it may sound far-fetched, but what you think, Gladys, after all you were friends with Kathleen Harriot, what you think?'

'It's hard to say, Alan. I just don't know, but my husband always said we should not rule out the place with its history and legacies, that it should also be taken into account. Geor-r-ge only came to that conclusion after he went to England and after the whole story with Kathleen Harriot... spent five yea-r-rs in

England... To this day I still don't know how he felt about that place. I think he remained neutral, but mind you that's only my opinion for I could never get a straight answer from that man. "Oh yes, Gladys," he used to say to me, "I can understand how a place can affect a person's life more than we think", those used to be his exact words. Then there was the matter of the light... was a big thing for him at that time... seems so long ago it's hard to believe it really happened. Where do the years go? Just imagine, I will be seventy-six in June, seventy-six, me, Gladys Davis... Anyway, as I was saying, he would keep on ha-a-rping about the day he returned, how when he stepped off the plane the light blinded him. I remember it took him weeks to readjust to it. The man would keep drawing the blinds in the house complaining the light was too ha-a-rsh for his eyes and I would complain that the lack of light acted like a pall on my spirits, that there was not enough light.

For a few weeks there was a constant pulling up and pulling down of blinds. It finally stopped when I broke my crystal vase that my mother had given me as a wedding gift. Geor-r-ge had pulled down the blinds as usual as soon as I had turned my back. I had dozed off and just gotten up, which made it worse... Anyway, to cut a long story short, my hand knocked down the vase and it fell and broke into little pieces. There was no chance of gluing it back, there were too many pieces to contend with. I don't think anything has ever upset me so much, even talking about it now still affects me. The blinds were drawn back from that moment. I told him he would either have to go blind or adjust again to the light, but I was not putting up with a house in constant darkness. Well, he eventually went to the optician, which he should have done in the first place... that was Mr. Bradley then wasn't it... Well anyway, it appeared he needed a pair of glasses, something to do with the glare... although I have to admit that he never fully recovered his sight until the time of Kathleen Harriot's granddaughter's departure to America...

but that's another story... but Geor-r-ge insisted that the day he came off the plane he could barely withstand it. In fact it was so bad that a fellow passenger from this same country who knew Geor-r-ge and was walking right behind him at the time thought something was the matter... can't remember the man's name... it's on the tip of my tongue... What was it again?... Small?... Smith?... Smart?... Anyway, whoever it was apparently approached Geor-r-ge and said , "Excuse me, Mr. Davis, but do you need any help?" And even put out his hand to Geor-r-ge as one would to a blind person. Geor-r-ge literally had to grope his way to the airport building. I remember wondering why in heaven's name he walked the way he did, as if feeling his way... his head was pushed forward, both of his hands stretched out before him as if he were playing a piano, and the thought did flash across my mind that he was drunk... not that he ever drank, mind you, for he was a godly man... but I knew how terrified he was of flying, was not at peace until his feet touched solid ground. As soon as he came up to me I remember asking him if something was wrong. "Geor-r-ge, you look so strange", I said to him, "just as if you can't see". "It's the light, Gladys," he kept saying... "What light?" I wanted to know. He kept saying that he would explain later, to leave him alone... He said it was only then it struck him, in a flash, how relentless this country is. Relentless heat, an intensity of colours, downpo-o-urs of rain. Just plain outpo-o-urings he used to say. I never quite understood him... So when it all happened, you know, with my old friend Kathleen Harriot claiming she was seeing cracks, with Kathleen's daughter, Stephanie, literally dying from a surfeit of love, and then Kathleen's granddaughter, Mar-r-garet, becoming ill from an overblown imagination and having to be sent away, Geor-r-ge wasn't at all surprised. Let me think... was it Mar-r-garet's brother Guy who accompanied her to America...? He's still over there and has no plans of returning according to their sister Adrienne... is a dentist and apparently doing very well... Yes, if I remember correctly, Guy was the one who accompanied Mar-r-garet to America for he was leaving to go to University at the same time she became ill. Adrienne took her sister's illness quite badly, which surprised everyone at the time for they never appeared to be very close... shows how one can never tell... From what I can gather Adrienne seems to have kept in constant contact with Mar-r-garet. I think she's the one who encouraged her to come back after all these years... twenty to be exact. Anyway, let me get back to the point and not digress on the ins and outs of that family or I would spend the next two days talking. As I was saying, Geor-r-ge felt that most of what happened was connected to this place with its history and legacies. After he returned he would insist that it is ha-a-rd to achieve a fine balance here, taking into account the imbalance that surrounds you. We dance all night, party all night, beat our women to death in jealous drunken rages, hate to death or love to death... there's no stopping us, Geor-r-ge used to say. We literally have to drop to our knees before we can put a halt to ourselves... "How could Stephanie be otherwise, Gladys!" he would argue with me. "Look at how she loved her husband Char-r-les Saunders from the moment they first met and would love him to the end... Would die of that love. As for Char-r-les, he couldn't have one or two or three women, no, he must have stre-e-ams of women, an excess of women... Women would have to be the death of him." Then he would refer to Kathleen herself, pointing out how much she loved her adopted son Compton. For Geor-r-ge, a love-seed was planted from the time the unknown woman arrived at Kathleen's home with Compton when he was only three days old. I can remember it was during the rainy season. In fact it had been raining for three days, so that didn't help much, for how could the seed not become sodden Geor-r-ge said... Yes, that was the word... sodden... still not quite clear as to what he meant and he didn't bother to explain... Kathleen's sister Irma, like John, never accepted Compton. I think it was the only time Irma Chase and John Harriot ever agreed on anything. Childless Irma, I used to think, was only envious, though she would never admit to that envy and John was as usual suspicious and distrustful of anything that for him was out of the ordinary. Seeds of doubt se-e-ethed in his mind from the very start, for to him Compton was an unknown quantity, brought in a strange way to his wife. It made no sense to him. I remember people used to think of him as a ha-a-rd man. According to Irma, Kathleen and John were two of a kind... they suited each other she used to say... but to give John his due, he also felt that their daughters, Stephanie and Eileen, were being brushed aside by their own mother for the sake of this boy. Kathleen was a dear-r friend, believe me, none of you here were as close to her as I was... dear-r Kathleen... such a strong woman in her time, yet who would have thought... changed so much... didn't allow herself to see *one* crack, as Geor-r-ge would point out to me just to prove his point, no she had to see one and two and three and four and five cracks until they overtook her. He became like a broken record when it came to this subject... yet in the end they seemed to see eye-to eye. They became closer, talked the same language. Then later, after the whole story, he would also go on and on about how he had started to see things afresh, how he began to read his country's legacies in a different light... was ha-a-rd to stop him... but there's no doubt he changed his ideas. I could hardly understand him sometimes, and believe me Geor-r-ge wasn't any great thinker, I can tell you... not one for books or ideas, just went about his daily business like most people. But one thing he kept saying to the end: that we need to look at our country's history in a new way... For him the whole thing was an eye-opener... like it seemed to be for Kathleen, no matter who thought otherwise... and George agreed with me. No matter what was said about her, I still say most people just didn't understand... Now Margaret's returning... after all these years... after all these years... '

'Gladys, who can say how it all started? It's so easy to see after the event, but when you yourself are part of it, that's another matter. As close as you were to them at the time, you were still an outsider... As the old saying goes, he who feels it knows it. Look at us, a group of old men and women sitting on your verandah talking about the past... that's all we ever do... talk about those who have passed on and the past... and it's not even as if we knew them as well as you did, but we did know something of them. Who didn't at the time? This country is small and Kathleen Harriot was well known. It was the talk of the town. It's okay to see what should or should not have been done from the outside, but when you're actually in the thing itself, now that's something else... Okay to talk about the place and the climate and the excess... but who knows, perhaps it would have happened wherever. Could have been in Timbuctu and it still would have occurred. Who knows... ?'

'I still feel it started with the cracks, but then I don't know as much about the whole thing as Gladys does. I only used to hear about it through my mother, who always made sure that nothing passed her. I used to tell her she should have been employed by the KGB... '

'To me, whether one knew the family well is not the point, and I certainly didn't. I worked for John Harriot but that was it... but it was the kind of story anyone could have an opinion on, and to me, from what I can gather, something must have led up to Kathleen Harriot thinking she was actually seeing her house literally crack up before her eyes. Things just don't appear out of the blue, there is always a connection, they don't just appear out of the blue sky.'

'Well, I don't know what any of you may think, but I still feel it was that house. There were always rumours and strange stories about that place. There was never any record of Kathleen Harriot's grandparents' burial... the only record was a verbal one of them fading fast. Think of it... two people having lived in a house so many years and no one, no one, could ever remember an actual funeral taking place. I remember her sister Irma kept repeating that the house should be smoked out, that unlaid-to-rest spirits were restless in that house and that her sister and husband should smoke it out. People keep forgetting the history of that house, but I never do. Gladys may have known Kathleen Harriot very well, but I used to visit Irma once in a while after Irma's husband Frank died... he was related to the Chases who once owned that jewellery store on Dapple Street. The son was named after the father, Frank William Chase... Irma and I used to attend the Pilgrim Holiness Church... she certainly helped to build up that Church... put a lot of work into it. We started off with about twelve people, including the Hopkins... They were the first American missionaries who came here from America to help found the Church. A few of the members found Irma to be bossy. They used to grumble about the way she made herself president for life of our Missionary Society. The first time Irma decided to hold a fair so as to raise some money to add a section to the church for the Bible Club, the Hopkins were quite upset and said it was no different to gambling. They even quoted from the Bible to prove their point. That didn't stop Irma Chase... She quoted back and said the Church needed money and a fair would be held... and so it was... she helped build that Church up from scratch, I can tell you.'

'Am... place, history, house, cracks, whatever it was... am... the thing is... the thing is... am... do we learn anything from it... anything... am...? Perhaps it would not have happened if they had started to pick up the pieces from way back and in the picking put them to good use... am... good use... The outburst must have been a result of so much being hidden for so long... you know what I mean... covered up... pasted over... am... now if something can be learned from it, then I would say it was not wasted... But was something learned? That's my point... am... that's my point... am... and excuse the digression, but I would like to say that Gladys refers to herself as being old... Well I choose to differ... am... to differ... I am seventy and still going strong... am... going strong... Who knows, I may yet pick up and marry some young girl and surprise all of you old fogies... '

'Eh, you do go on don't you, all of you. Is all too much for my ole brain because I'm ole and I jus' don't know. There's never any easy answers. My husban' says wasn't our business anyway. He thinks that's the problem... If people had only minded their business, a lot of what happened could've been avoided... but he says we never learn, we keep on like nothing ever happen. At the beginning opinions fly up and down, then we go home and faget... lose intrest and feed on something else. He says our attention span's too short... and why this intrest in Kathleen Harriot and her family all of a sudden? For years people seemed to faget and now here we are bringing up that ole story jus' because Kathleen granddaughter Margaret returning... '

'Talking 'bout names, maybe that's where the whole thing start... think 'bout it... Maybe we should've put a name to it. We should've given this country a name... this would've helped... A place without a name can't come to terms with itself. All that burning and looting and slaughtering of each other because of affiliatshuns to diff'rent political parties might never have started in the first place if we could only have put a name to it...'

'Ahmm... excuse me, but I'm going home. Gladys is right... none of us knew dhat family dhe way she did. We were only acquaintances going by rumours and hearsay. I remember vaguely seeing Katleen Harriot's daughters Stephanie... and what was dhe other one's name... oh yes, Eileen. I remember seeing dhem once in a while when dhey would go into town... Dhey were both smart dressers so one couldn't help noticing dhem... Dhe adopted son, Compton, always struck me as a resentful young lad, didn't seem to fit in wid dhe family, always gave me dhe impression of being an outsider... and I have to agree wid Gladys dhat Katleen Harriot seemed to love Compton more dhan her own two daughters, but at dhe same time wasn't she very hard wid him? At least dhat's the feeling I got whenever I heard her speak to him. She seemed to be quite domineering... ahmm... Anyway I'm tired... it's too hot to go into all of dhis highfaluting talk... you notice... not a bret of air... It's no different to my son who's always talking about some 'ism' or some 'ology'. Somebody he knows is always studying some 'ology'... Dhere he goes and christens his daughter wid some kind of name dhat I can't even pronounce. "Why can't you call her someting simple like Joan or Tracy or Marilyn? Why a name I can't even remember, much less pronounce?" I guess by talking we feel we've come to some understanding at our ages, but if you want to call a spade a spade, I don't tink we understand much of what went on... ahmm... Some of you here were once school teachers, so you sound no different to textbooks but I was just a housewife and like Gladys' husband George not one for book learning. Names and ambushes and low lying memories and legacies and history are too much for me... it's all too much. I can't afford to tink too much at my age. I have to hold on to what I've been taught all my life. It's enough to deal wid my granddaughter's name. I can't afford to disrupt all I know or I might end up seeing cracks myself. Let me deal wid what I know... too old to look into anyting else... would only lead to pure confusion. Perhaps dhat was Katleen Harriot's trouble and why she began to see cracks. At her ripe old age she began to see someting else and instead of letting it lie low she began to investigate and pry... Dhat's where she got into trouble. She should've left dhe cracks alone and dhey would've disappeared, but no, she decided to investigate and get to dhe source... What could you expect na? Let me go home. For me... I will let sleeping collared dogs lie... ahmm...'

CHAPTER TWO

It was just as the clock struck six and Kathleen Harriot turned over on her bed and opened her eyes that she happened to notice, from where she lay, what appeared to be a deep crack on the wall facing her. It took her a few seconds to collect herself. The light in the bedroom was still dim as the blinds were drawn. She thought it strange if it was indeed a crack. Perhaps it was a trick of the light, perhaps a trick of the eyes; one could never tell.

She groped for her glasses on the bedside table. Ah, here they were, next to the Bible. She carefully put them on and once again cast her eyes to the wall. Yes, she could now see a lot clearer, except for the usual finger marks on the glasses. She must remember to clean them or ask Margaret, as lately the child seemed to enjoy doing it. She would creep up from behind her and gently remove them from her face so as not to make her jump at the sudden movement. 'Grandmother let me clean your glasses'... 'I've always wanted to ask you, Mrs. Harriot, you're called Grandmother by your grandchildren, but what do they call your sister?' Mrs. Talbot asked that just yesterday when she passed by to see how she was doing... considerate woman... Over the years would occasionally stop by to look in on her, though not a close family friend. 'My sister is called Granny Irma by Stephanie's children and Eileen's daughter, even though she's their great-aunt... Don't know who decided on it... Sometimes one can never tell how or when things are started'... Like getting old, like yesterday when Adrienne was combing her hair for the tea party at the YWCA. As Adrienne pulled the hair away from her face she caught a view of herself in the mirror and in a flash saw the scrawled lines, the pulled-down, pulled-at flesh, the face of an old woman, a residue of time. She pulled away for a moment in this tug-of-time, not daring to look, as if by this act she could blot it out. But then she pulled-up her face again to the mirror hopeful hoping, and this time saw the wrung-out, roped neck. As she fell back she murmured to the room, 'My neck looks no different to a turkey's, doesn't it? Our mother used to tell us it was the first sign. The face may pass but the neck is the give away.' The years had shuffled up from all sides and she had given it the barest attention. Insidiously they had scraped themselves across her flesh, dragged themselves across her flesh, pulled and nagged at her flesh eventually beating it down. At that moment she blamed the mirror, she blamed the light, she blamed the day, for after all, 'there are days and days and this was just one of them. There are mirrors and mirrors,' she murmured; 'it all depends on the light. Nothing more than the neck of a turkey.'

'Did your mother Hope Amelia Robertson say that the neck is the first sign? Is that what she said, Grandmother?' And then the child laughed, came up to the mirror and looked, then she laughed. 'What are you laughing at, Margaret; it will happen to you one day. I know it's hard for you to believe, as you are still fettered by youth as I am by age, but one day it will happen and you won't even see it happening... takes you by surprise...'

The child nodded as if she understood and for a moment looked just as careworn as the old woman... curious child... Now why did she call out her mother's name like that as if invoking it? Hope Amelia Robertson. In fact, when she thought of it, there were instances like this one when it was just as if Iris were back with her, instances of stark recognition that came and went in the flicker of an eyelid. Irma always said it, always said Margaret reminded her of their sister Iris... Was it the expression, the gesture of the hands, the turn of the head, the furtive look as if she were up to something, the way she was always into a book, couldn't leave the printed word alone, pursuing it relentlessly? Or perhaps it was the eyes scrutinizing the word, the very soul leaving one with a feeling of unease, just like Iris used to do... the one who in pursuing the word never seemed to care to pursue marriage or friendship or anything for that matter. 'Haven't you found anyone yet?' their mother would ask, never letting go. 'You are far too choosy... We have not had any old maids in the family. You can't only seek words, you must also set your sights on marriage and having children. A woman should get married and have children. Pick and choose the way you do and you will end up with the bramble, mark my words.'

Iris always walked alone, was the one always to be sought, later to be found, most likely under a tree buried in the leaves of a book...

'It isn't natural the reading she does and yet one can hardly get a word out of her,' their mother would complain. 'Mumbles her way through life... For a girl she reads too much, will fill her head with pure book knowledge, but that isn't enough for a woman. Leave that to your brothers; they will have families to support.'

Iris, who was called the dark one, not as fair as the others, the one who took after the father... Iris, whom their mother had considered as someone in hiding what from she could never tell, in hiding like any common criminal going about like a thief in the night, no one daring to say that their mother also gave the feeling of being on the alert as she tiptoed her way through the house, slid along walls, gripped bannisters as if for dear life in anticipation... who for all of her married life would use only one chair, refusing to sit on any other, never allowing her bedroom door or windows to be opened more than a crack. At any strange sound she would jump-up and yet would jump down Iris's throat for acting like a person in hiding, yet she herself had remained in hiding for years, waiting for a white man, any white man once he was a white man...

Iris, the one who continued to live alone in their parents' house after their deaths, never to step out of it again until death stepped in and took a hand. She would drive their father so mad that he would beat her as if she were one of his own sons with strong enough backs to bear the blows, the cane whistling through the air. 'I'll beat the fear of God into you if it's the last thing I do,' and she would accept them as if they were her due without a cry, which would make their father strike even harder to elicit that cry, anything rather than the silence, the acceptance, as if this were nothing else but her due. 'I'm the one in charge of this household and you will not forget it... You will not escape it, not while I am in this house.'

Their father, proudly referred to as Mr. Albert Fred Robertson by the villagers, since he was the first negro headmaster of the village school, a man who extended the role onto his family. A harsh, strict man who firmly believed that if one spared the rod one spoiled the child... his only restraints his God and then his wife. A man who dared to remove and marry the woman who could pass for white from under the very eyes of her parents was seen as a man who walked tall and stood tall though standing no more than 5' 7", who feared no man, not even the white man... His wife, a woman whose only claim was that she could pass for white, at least in this unnamed country where it was hinted one could pass for anything if one had the know-how, for in other places she would be in the same boat as most of them, but to her parents, Robert Gerald Hinckson and Cecilia Margaret Hinckson, what further proof could one extract from the white man but the case of a mistaken identity, since their daughter from the time of her birth had been mistaken for white by the white doctor himself and for this very reason given the name Hope.

What further evidence did one need, her parents would stress? So in the passing she was taught that she had the right to be considered as one, accepted as one. But however one looked at it, they pointed out, however one looked, from whatever angle one viewed it, it gave her an advantage in this country and in the outside world... She was already ahead of the race.

Taught by her parents from very early that in the passing she was already eligible to be the future bride of some white man, any white man, once he was a white man. Taught that her chances were that high ever since she was that high. But in the teaching it was concluded, after what was later considered much deliberation and weighing of words and thoughts based on experience, that her history be blanked out as this might prove to be an encumbrance that she could ill afford to carry along with her, a whole lot of grip-filled pain, and he who might eventually have to come to grips with having married a woman of false identity could not be expected to take on any other additional baggage, which at the most unexpected moments might turn up, forcing her to have to sit on it, press down hard it on to keep all that stuff from breaking out. No, they sputtered with such vehemence, that even those who heard were surprised, as they were mainly seen as a retiring couple. One man said later that they shouted so loud to make their point the spit flew out of their mouths and spattered the onlookers' faces. No, every possible loophole had to be covered so as to give their daughter the chance to go to some white man with a blank slate, and very few had the advantage of starting all over again with a blank slate. For why was she christened Hope from the moment the white people kept mistaking her for white and assuming her mother to be nursemaid, but for the hope of their race? For she could be the means of wiping out forever the pain and suffering they had been made to endure from the very moment their great great great grandparents were ambushed and violently shackled and collared and dumped together like heaps of blind coal, all chain-bound, all slave-bound, but some also fear-bound, hate-bound, suicide-bound, slaughter-bound, sullen-bound, survive-at-all-costs-bound, blank-look-bound, blank-out-bound, despair-bound, amnesia-bound, tractable-bound, black-out-bound, run-amok-bound, word-bound, hope-bound, maroon-bound, spirit-bound, god-bound but all chain-bound, all slave-bound, bound to the point of no return on ships steered by men who lacked colour and by that very lack were given the means to be members of the human race while they, because of their stained skins, were made more visible and so sold and designated as human beasts of burden at a place that no one could ever put a name to. Bound together by history, but where did that get them... So was it wrong to see their Hope as the means of unbinding by binding her to any white man? And was their suffering not now even greater due to a very lack of endurance? Had they not now gotten to the breaking point, the point of no return? So how could they not help but rest their hopes on her, this daughter of theirs, who by the very fact of a mistaken identity could be the means of removing the stained skin and history for future generations by marrying some colourless man, any colourless man, once he was not a man of colour?

    No, every possible loophole had to be covered and they looked into their fear-eaten selves and understood from that moment that they would also have to be covered over, for were they not proof of her history and was not this proof to be blanked-out at all costs? And so for the sake of their daughter's future marriage, for the sake of future generations, they, from that moment, gradually began to erase themselves from her memory slate, leaving her in the hands of an old servant woman. They must have faded fast, she told her children later, for in a short while they became so inconspicuous that one could bump into them anywhere and not realise.

And as they began to erase themselves, she was soon after removed to a room, later called the waiting room, in which she would remain locked-in until a white man, any white man, some white man passed through the village and in the passing would ask for her hand.

On the few occasions when some white man would pass through requiring a place to stay, to rest his head, the villagers would point out the two-storeyed house that stood behind the two coconut trees, at the same time telling the stranger, as they accompanied him, of how this house was passed on by a childless old white mistress to the couple who now lived there, Robert Gerald Hinckson married to one Cecilia Margaret Hinckson, who begat one daughter Hope Amelia Hinckson, passed on to them on 1 May 1850 when their old childless white mistress, while receiving the sacrament of extreme unction, was so driven to extremity that clots of guilt dropped out of her, splashed all over her, making her howl for the couple who carried her name, who were once a part of her property, howl that they be dragged up if necessary to her death bed with their daughter to be willed, by the will of God, the two-storeyed house standing behind two coconut trees, willed before she dropped out of this life. And so, Hope Amelia Hinckson would be escorted down the stairs without a word by the servant woman to eat with the white stranger, and without a word be taken back up to her room, and he would not even bother to explain – for why should he being white? – that he was only passing through, would be gone before cock crow. So her time passed, her parents already fading for what they claimed was the perpetuation of their race which through Hope's marriage would make them eligible once again to be members of the human race since they, by a stroke of fate or curse, or by greed-driven men or power-driven men or by violent-driven men or heartless men or by will of God or history or proclamation or whatever, had once been made into human beasts of burden and she, through the consumation of a marriage, could remove all at once in the stroke of a pen the stain and beast, so as to give them the chance to re-enter the human race.

So her time shuffled by, until one night she heard the stranger's voice beneath her window. It was a man's voice but not a white man's voice. She later claimed her husband to be a man of great persuasion, for was he not able to woo her out of that room on that fateful night, which at the time caused a great sensation in the country? Albert Fred Robertson, the man who would later ride up to the Governor's House in a donkey cart demanding to see the Governor and would not leave until he had done so to demand pensions for the teachers, a man who was able to speak with such persuasive conviction and passion that the Governor himself bombarded the very teachers who had been afraid to support his demand, which also caused a sensation, a man who was said to fear no man including the white man, a man more to be feared than God, for at least that fear was unseen.

He called out, 'I know you for a good while, lady who pass for white. You think you hide away in that room and nobody can see you, but I catch glimpses of you through your window. I listen to you moving about your room. I feel the loneliness you feel lock up in that room all these years, waiting for some white man to come along and take you away as his bride. Well, listen carefully to what I have to tell you because I will not speak to you again. Is hardly likely any white man will ever marry you. He will have to be a very special kind of man and is not easy to find special kind of men whatever the colour. And even if you marry that special kind of man you still negro. No marriage can remove your history, no matter what they tell you. You going to carry that history with you wherever you go and no matter how you press down hard hard it going to come out. Lady, who they say can pass for white, listen to me. I want to marry you. I know you better than anybody else. Better to marry me, a negro man, than to die in that room for the sake of an illusion. You going to fade away even faster than your parents for the sake of a hard-to-come-by white man. I will come every night and wait under this window for you. I will not speak to you again. Is for you to weigh my words and decide. I hope is not too late by the time you do so, lady who pass for white...'

So that was how she began to crochet what later no one could ever put a name to, 'but I took the pattern off of the spider's web which floated above my bed,' their mother would later spill out to them the day after her husband's burial and two weeks before she died... the web which had gradually begun to spread itself over the years and which no one cared to sweep away.

As the crochet work progressed so did the spider's web. She worked rapidly to overtake it, sometimes spending sleepless nights doing so. Then one day she caught up with it. She spread the intricate criss-crossed lines of thread across the floor. It floated for a while lighter than a breath. She slept soundly that night for the first time in months, but when she awoke the following morning she saw immediately that the spider had once again moved ahead, had obviously worked long hours through the night. The web had spread so rapidly it already covered part of the wall and was moving towards her bed. She worked in a frenzy for the next few days but it was of no use, she could not keep up with the spider.

When she awoke the next morning, in a panic-stricken moment she thought she had gone blind, for it was as if she were caught in a whirlpool of delicate wraiths of smoke. She reached out her hand to feel her way and only then realised that the spider's web was now draped over her bed like a mosquito net. She called out to the servant not to leave her any food that day. She lay under the web without moving, her hands folded over her breasts and waited for nightfall. The web was closing in, she knew it. Its web-fingers were already reaching out towards her. They fanned her face gently, stroked her face gently, fluttered over her face gently, lighter than a breath. 'It's hardly likely a white man will ever marry me,' she whispered. 'I may pass for white, but passing does not make me white. If a white man ever marries me he will have to be a special kind of man and there are few special men of any colour. I will fade away from sight and memory like my parents have done for the sake of something that is worthless. Better to take the luggage than die in this room, better to accept the luggage than fade away from memory and sight.'

She suddenly sprang up and tried to cast the web off. It wasn't easy. She sensed that there was little time left. She could hardly breathe as the fingers caught at her hair, her face, her hands, rippled over her hair, her face, her hands, but she fought it off, clawed at it, tore at it, ripped it away and was finally freed of it. It was almost daybreak; she knew there was little time left. The fingers floated behind her, stroking her hair, pulling her gently backwards. She paused only for a moment, then grabbed the crocheted web and, running to the window, cast it out. For a moment she felt nothing and her heart fluttered. Then she felt the pull, the drag of it. Without a backward glance she climbed onto the mango tree outside the window and worked her way down. And so she found her future husband lying beneath the tree, tangled up in her web of crochet made according to a spider's design. She had to tear it away as he floundered beneath it. And so they fled and were married at daybreak by a drunken white minister who disappeared that same day, never to be seen again... she wrapped in her web of crochet, strands of the spider's web still lightly floating over her face in a transparent veil of grey... he a black man who dared ask for the hand of this woman who passed for white, at least in this part of the world, with only his bold-faced colour, bold-faced daring and bold-faced ambition to offer, and she, a pale-faced woman who dared accept, with only her web of crochet and her white pass to offer, never to bump into her parents again, at least not on this earth, never to receive a written record of their burial, only that they had faded even faster after her departure... this woman, Hope Amelia Hinckson, of Dutch and African ancestry married a man of African ancestry, Albert Fred Robertson, and bore him six children: three daughters, Iris Ethel, Kathleen Maud, and Irma Augusta and three sons, Stanley Ian, Christopher Michael and Percival Matthew.

'... I will put the fear of God into you if it's the last thing I do.' Iris... break... crack... what was it she was going to do? Oh yes, the wall... mother... father... web... now what in the world brought on all that... things that were long done with. She hadn't thought of them for such a long time she later told her friend, Gladys Davis. She said to her that it was just as if the whole thing took place right before her, as if the crack had opened up its lips and the whole thing spilled out the same way it had once spilled out from her mother's own lips the day after she buried her husband, Alfred Fred Robertson, and would continue to spill out until she died two weeks later and was laid by his side. She said to Gladys Davis she couldn't explain it, was at a loss for words to do so, for she had never ever had such an experience, she said to her, and hoped never to have it again... for it was almost as if she had actually caught a glimpse of her sister Iris... and all because of a simple crack. She was a meticulous woman when it came to her house, the only one not willed to her by her now-dead husband, John Harriot, once a man of property if not looks, said her sister... a man of the world which she, Irma Augusta Chase, was not a part of and would not be a part of since the day of her salvation.

She removed the blanket from her body, put on her slippers which lay by the bed and shuffled across the wooden floor to the wall. She grabbed at her hip as she felt the surge of pain. 'I'm getting old,' she thought, as if the realization suddenly struck her for the first time before remembering yesterday. She was slowing down, no doubt about it. Just recently at the bank she noticed how she was beginning to lose control over her hands when she tried to sign her name. The letters seemed to stagger across the paper onto the very edge of the line. However well they said she looked, however strong the beat of her heart, she could feel the difference.

Her eyes were now more accustomed to the light. Without looking up she knew his eyes were looking down directly at her from the wall. The picture he insisted be taken three days after their wedding. The eyes that refused to let her go. Insisting, insisting... 'Kathleen, that boy will make you grieve, can't you see it...? Remember your two daughters. They deserve just as much attention, if not more. You are doing too much for him and he isn't worth it, can't you see?' 'You will never give up, John, will you?' she said to him. 'Even death itself couldn't take that away from you, even death itself.'

She could hear Mrs. Wood in her kitchen next door from the sound of the running pipe water while the cock crowed just as she got to the wall. No doubt about it, it was indeed a crack. She put out her hand tentatively and gently pulled her finger across it as if she were stroking a lover's lips to confirm the spoken word was not a lie. The cock crowed once again. She returned to her bed and her body sank down onto the mattress. The face flesh staggered. Strange, she thought, as she stretched her hand out towards the Bible. The arm flesh staggered. Strange, since there was no crack there when she went to her bed the evening before, she was certain of that. She remembered turning on the radio as usual at nine pm to listen to the death announcements and the shock of hearing of her friend Ruby's death. She remembered calling downstairs to Irma, 'Irma, Irma, did you hear that Ruby is dead? What a thing!' But Irma had already heard for she was also calling, 'Kathleen, Kathleen, did you hear that, Ruby is dead.'

Poor Ruby, having to be taken to that old people's home was the death of her... her pride couldn't stand it. Ruby, who had borne seven children, yet left alone without the means to take care of herself or have someone take care of her in her old age, so having to be taken to an old people's home. The children scattered abroad, America, England; she heard one was even in Ethiopia. All of them scattered like their own two brothers, Christopher and Percival, who left for America immediately after their parents' death. But that was their fate... to leave the country whatever the race: black, white, chinese, whatever, to leave as soon as they could to what was considered better opportunities. Psalm 25... she leafed through the pages.

She was indeed a meticulous woman who took great care of this house, passed on in an extreme moment of guilt to her mother's parents by a childless white woman and then to her own mother since there was no written record of her parents' burial, only a verbal one of them fading fast... Iris its only occupant until death stepped in and took charge, and then to her, Kathleen Harriot, because she had possessed the means to have it delivered board by board and rebuilt according to the original design. So she thought of the crack... at least fifteen inches. She thought of the bill... at least twenty dollars, if not more. She thought of the carpenter, Mr. Carlton... must speak with Mr. Carlton today, let him have a look. She thought of her taxes... she must remember to remind Stephanie to take the cheque to the Ministry on her way to work. She thought of Ruby, poor Ruby, having to be taken to the old people's home with no family left to look after her, a woman who had borne seven children, but what good did that do her in the end? She thought of how she would hate having to be taken to an old people's home because she didn't have the means to take care of herself or have someone take care of her.

That fear would sometimes weigh fearfully on her very soul. It would surge up at the most unexpected moments. Could be in the middle of a dinner as she was about to put a forkful of rice into her mouth, or at church in the middle of a prayer or on the bus as she looked out of the window and saw an old man walking by. It could happen anywhere with no respect for time or place. It would drag at the strings of her heart, replaying the same old fears of an aging woman. Suppose she lost all her money, had no one to look after her, was helpless... suppose?

How could any of them understand how important it was to have this house, a roof over her head, not beholden to anyone, enough money to be looked after until her death, enough money to take care of her burial. They couldn't understand or didn't seem to care to do so, unable to see the Rubies. Instead, they all relied on her and the money they imagined she must have lying dormant in the bank, money which her now-dead husband must have left her, which she never spoke of. The fact she never spoke of it must mean there was something to hide. Only the other day she heard Eileen talking to Stephanie about her, telling Stephanie that she was a frugal woman who held on too tightly to her money and considering she had so much... that she must have... for then why would she keep her bank-book hidden... there had to be a reason... and considering that they were her daughters, yet had received very little after their father's death but instead most of it had been given to Compton... he had received it all... that it was not fair and had never been fair... everything gone to Compton except for this old house... Stephanie, as usual, just murmured ... apart... not really caring since the day her own husband Charles informed her of his final departure, and she not daring to acknowledge the reason, only nailed to the moment, unable to remove herself from that moment.

These were trying times. None of them listened. If it weren't for Gladys it would be very difficult... the only person she could truly rely on since the death of John... Psalm 25... 'Here it is, I must mark the spot so I won't always have this trouble to find it,' she murmured. 'I say it, yet I never do so... Unto thee oh Lord do I lift up my soul... Oh my God I trust in thee... turn thee unto me and have mercy upon me... for I am desolate and afflicted... the troubles of my heart are enlarged...' She heaved her body onto the floor and knelt by the bed. She had to pause to catch her breath before she could speak... 'Dear God,' she prayed very softly, and the words buzzed in the quiet of the morning throughout the house like an air raid of mosquitoes, 'Come to our aid. Be with the ones who are scattered abroad, keep them safe.' Her daughter Stephanie in the room next to hers stretched and yawned... Time to get up... time to start getting ready for work... time to wake-up the children... The young boy lay on his back, his eyes trailing the roach as it crawled across the ceiling. His body tensed as he thought of the math exam... 'Remember Guy in his exam today, help him Oh Lord for he has studied hard. Thank you for the blessings we have received. Amen...'

I moved my eye away from the crack in the wall and quietly replaced the picture over it. My sister Adrienne was still asleep. I could hear my brother Guy tossing about on his bed. My mother was getting up. I could hear her. I am Margaret Saunders... Call me the eavesdropper.

CHAPTER THREE

Perhaps my grandmother would have let it pass since the carpenter, Mr. Carlton, did not come to the house until five days later. Perhaps she would have let it pass, let the crack remain, after all it was just a crack and perhaps it was there all the time but it was only because of her deterioriating eyesight, her failing memory that she had forgotten about it... perhaps... But when a second one appeared on the following day, just above the first, and a third one the following day after that, and then a fourth and fifth how was it possible to let it pass? So when Mr. Carlton came she took him straight to her bedroom.

'There, Mr. Carlton, five cracks over the past five days. Now how is that possible? Where in heaven's name can they be coming from? This house is well kept up as you know. It is like new, so why these cracks, tell me?'

'Look all right to me, Miss Harriot. Don' see anyting wrong.'

'What in heaven's name do you mean, Mr. Carlton? There are these deep cracks, five of them, right before our very eyes and you tell me you don't see anything wrong? Are you telling me I'm blind.'

'No, Miss Harriot, but... hmm... a jus' sayin' it look all right to me. Maybe we can wait and see how dhe situation go first before we do anyting about it.'

'Well?' Aunt Eileen asked as soon as Mr. Carlton left the

room. 'Well? What did my mother say and what do you think? Did you see anything or is something wrong with me? Tell me the truth, Mr. Carlton, because I know you have worked with her for years and have a soft spot for her. You've worked with her long enough. We know her as a practical, sensible woman, so what do you think of these cracks she is apparently seeing?'

'Hmmm... A have to agree with you dhis time, Miss Eileen. A really didn't see anyting.'

'Yuh shouldn't tell her so,' Rose said to him. 'Yuh mus' go along wid her. Miss Harriot gettin' old. Wid Mr. Harriot dead all dhese years, an' she lef' alone to manage and dhen dhe bad way Mr. Compton treat her... Dhen Miss Stephanie so unhappy and I know she blamin' herself for dhat... is too much fuh her at her age. Widout her dhis family would all be on dhe street, everyone a dhem includin' me. As fuh Miss Chase, she blame her sister fuh everyting, but where would she be widout dhis house? Is who bring me from dhe country when my fadder couldn't manage wid all his chil'ren after my mudder die? Dhen look at all dhe years my husban' in dhe bush workin' as a pork knocker lookin' fuh gold, scratchin' fuh gold. He go dhere widout even tinkin' what is to happen to me his wife. You tink dhat man ever lis'en to me when a tell him he wastin' his time lookin' fuh gold. Is better to look fuh work dhan spen' yuh time in dhe bush where anyting can just take yuh life... snake, tiger, spider, anyting... but he never lis'en... just get catch up in dhis gold fever and is only because of Miss Harriot... wid all her ways, 'cause a not sayin' she an angel, 'cause of her I have somewhere to lay my head at night... Whatever dhey say 'bout her I'm tankful fuh what she do fuh me and I will not faget it. Yuh shoulda go along wid her. Don't follow dhat Miss Eileen. Her life in a big enough mess. She is dhe las' person I would lis'en to.'

'But a didn't see any crack dhere, Rose. You yuhself say so. What yuh expect me to do?'

'Go along wid her, Ah say. She gettin' old. Go along wid her... What is dhat a hearin'? Well, if is not Margaret herself hidin' in dhe cupboard, listenin' to every word we sayin'. Dhis chile is too much. Don' let nuttin' pass her. Now you get out a dhis kitchen and don' lemme catch you in here again.'

...But suppose it's true, Arabella? Suppose your nose is a door post... suppose? Oh, but how can I expect anything from you at this point, you've only recently arrived. I keep forgetting that... one month to be exact... How can I expect the little I've been telling you of this family to be enough for you to have an opinion. I mean, even I am only now getting to know you... The cracks are there as my grandmother says and they've started making her remember all sorts of things she had thought long dead and buried, yet no one else in the house can see them. Look... look at the bubbles... ooh... that's a big one, there, just look at the colours, no different to the pretty colours you wear... Look, look... there we are in that one, the two of us, Margaret and Arabella, on the step just like a picture. Oh I wish I had a camera. Guy has one but he never lets me use it. But my mother can't afford it so I won't ask her... Look at us... we're going up, up inside of the bubble, up, up... and away... There we are over the fence into Mr. Wood's yard... floating away... pop! We're gone... it landed on the ginnip tree... we're gone... disappeared into thin air. Adrienne says I should grow up... Met Shirley Smith from my school and couldn't believe we're in the same class... says why can't I be like Shirley because she's so grown up, that she already has a boyfriend... thinks I'm so childish... blowing bubbles is for children. My cousin Norma agrees with her... But you like it don't you, Arabella... bubbles of colour just hanging in the air on an invisible christmas tree. I think Christmas is the best time of the year except for Easter. I'm definitely going to make my own kite this year. I'm also going window-shopping this year. I love to hear the Christmas carols and see the stores lit up with the most beautiful packages laid out there just for the taking...They must be for the taking for why would Santa, sitting behind the window, beckon and smile, swaying backwards and forwards, backwards and forwards murmuring, 'Come in, come in it's all for the taking'... I'm sure that's what he's saying, all laid out for the taking, if it weren't for the glass... Anyway, Arabella, I will try and take you this year if they will only let me...

'Margaret, Margaret, oh there you are... Come here at once. You haven't touched your lunch. Adrienne and Guy and Norma ate ages ago... What are you doing? Don't tell me you're sitting there playing with bubbles... When are you going to grow up child? I keep telling you you're no longer nine or ten years old... you should be showing an interest in other things; it's not healthy... I keep telling Stephanie this... Get up from there at once... Now just look at your clothes, how filthy they are... mud all over... I don't know what's to happen to you... I just don't know,' Aunt Eileen shouted.

CHAPTER FOUR

A voice was heard calling one late afternoon, a voice which none could lay claim to afterwards.

'Close the door, child, quick close the door... a funeral passing. I keep telling you children to always keep the door closed, but who listens... Sometimes I feel I'm talking to a brick wall... enough trouble pass through the house already without adding more... Is enough to invite trouble but to invite death is too much. I didn't say to slam the door, child, I said to close it. No need to slam it like that, no need whatsoever.'

'What was that noise, Rose?' my mother asked. 'You heard it... like the slam of a door?'

'Yes, Miss Saunders, make me jump, I was wonderin' myself.'

'What did it sound like to you?'

'Just like yuh say, like a door slam.'

'Go and see what it is. I will check the rice.'

Rose entered the drawing room and saw Uncle Ralph sitting in the rocking chair as she had left him some hours before, the same rocking chair he took out of the storeroom and mended and polished and then used from the time he first came to live with my grandmother and grandfather two years after they were married and one year after my mother was born. On 1 June 1916 he arrived at my grandparents' doorstep with one bag in his hand. On 2 June 1916 he went into the storeroom and took out that old rocking chair that no one even remembered. There was so much dust Granny Irma said he sneezed for hours. He would rock and rock and rock on the old rocking chair... but this time there was no rocking... Instead his head was dragged back as if an invisible hand held it; his Adam's apple jutted out like a rock. His eyes were fixed on the ceiling with such intensity that Rose automatically looked up. She couldn't help herself as if for one instant the same hand stretched out towards her and also jerked her head backwards. For days after she complained about her stiff neck and the pain, walked around for days after with her head on her shoulder. Rose screamed and couldn't say why, but she insisted she couldn't help herself. Later she claimed that the slam was death itself entering the house. She now says she felt goosebumps when she heard that sound because it was not of this earth, that it was terrifying when she felt the pull. 'What pull?' Aunt Eileen exclaimed. She feels Rose has always been too dramatic and her head is filled with too much nonsense and she's been filling my head with the same nonsense, instead of Rose cleaning the house the way she should, since that is her job, to clean and cook and wash, she told Granny Irma... Only yesterday Aunt Eileen said she noticed how much dust was under the chairs and the piano in the flat where she and my cousin Norma and Granny Irma live... that the house needed a good cleaning and when she said house, she meant all three flats... but instead Rose spent her time talking with Mr. Carlton and filling my head with pure nonsense... and another thing Aunt Eileen felt she should mention, as she has mentioned so often, was the way Rose dressed... She feels Rose should wear a white cap and apron... it looks better she insists... instead Rose dressed as if she were not a servant... She's been warning my mother but as usual she ignores her.

I asked Arabella what she thought about the death-pull Rose insists she felt, for she should have some kind of opinion by now considering she had been brought to my grandmother's house just before the cracks started appearing. I told her she must have picked up a few hints on this household by now, not forgetting the little bits here and there I've been filling her in with, (seeing none of them had taken the time or even cared to do so), she should have some kind of opinion. But as usual Arabella didn't answer. But I believed Rose. Why then would she take to her bed, as my grandmother said, for two days? Two whole days... take to her bed, and in all the years she knew her, Rose had never been sick one day. That says something doesn't it, Arabella? And all because of a door not being closed.

It was the shock, Granny Irma said, that made her take to her bed. There was no sign of anything. Uncle Ralph got up at daybreak as usual, had a good breakfast as usual and even told Grandmother he might take a walk later in the morning. The death was like a slap in the face, but then wasn't it invited in like a guest, Granny Irma insisted. It was given an open invitation after all. Even death itself must have been taken by surprise at the open invitation and what else could it do but take the first person that came along and there he was, my grandfather's brother of good health and strong mind, sitting on his usual chair by the stairs as if waiting for a visitor.

Grandmother didn't take to her bed but she took to her room and remained in there for about six hours. 'She's grieving,' Aunt Eileen said authoritatively. Rose just hissed her teeth and walked out of the dining room when she said that. She doesn't like Aunt Eileen... has never said it, but I can tell. I went to my mother's room next to Grandmother's and tried to hear her grieving. I pressed against the wall straining my ears to pick up something, but all I could hear was plop plop plop... just like that.

I was tempted to climb on the bed and look over the wall to see what it was, but I decided against it. 'She's grieving,' Aunt Eileen repeated, 'and refuses to cry in public, at least has not done since Daddy's death and Compton's departure. It's the shock. You know, one minute here, the next gone. It's not easy and she's getting old. Why next year she's going to be seventy-six. God, the years are flying. Look at Margaret, already fourteen and I can still remember her as a baby... now she's into everybody's business.'

I have to admit this time I went away empty handed. I could pick up nothing except for the plopping sound. Come to think of it, neither do I get even a screech from you, Arabella... perhaps you are also grieving... who knows? Aunt Eileen says she can't understand why Granny Irma would ever take it on herself to bring you here, that you are from the bush where the stupid buck people come from. I felt like telling her she was the stupid one, for the first time I felt like telling her just that. She thinks I spend too much time with you, just like I used to with Rose until you came along... She says she can't understand the types I seem to want to associate with, thinks because you don't say anything that you are stupid, but then birds of a feather flock together she says... But don't take what she says too seriously. If she heard me telling you this she would slap me and say, 'Hush up, Margaret, don't answer back, you know too much for your own good'... Yet at the same time she considers me childish...Why can't I have friends like my sister Adrienne? Adrienne's different that's why... just as you're different. I think you're just tongue-tied like I get when I'm with strangers... and we're strangers to you aren't we... or perhaps you've been hushed up... that's it... Perhaps someone slapped you *whoosh* right across your mouth and told you to hush up... It's either one or the other... tongue-tied or hushed up... right?

CHAPTER FIVE

My grandmother cared very much for Uncle Ralph, the brother of her now-dead husband, John Albert Harriot, seeing he lived with them soon after their marriage. He himself never got married, visited the same woman every day for twenty-five years but never married her. They would openly sit on the verandah for all to see so everyone knew about it... He never spoke about it so it was never verbally acknowledged and when she died three months ago he became very silent... At the stroke of midnight she apparently sprang straight up on her bed and called out loudly, then fell back, so by the time the woman who lived with her all those years got to the room she was already dead... He continued to take his usual walks in the afternoons but became very silent... He wanted to join her, Rose said, she could see it in his eyes. Uncle Ralph spent years with my grandparents, Arabella... was there from the time their two daughters, Aunt Eileen and my mother, were born... remained here at this house for forty-five years... just think of it, Arabella... that's such a long long time... that's old. I'm only telling you all of this to give you an introduction. None of them took the time out to do so... They tell you to have manners and yet none of them even bothered to introduce you... Well I did. They just brought you here and there I saw you as I was coming in from school. If you can remember, I immediately introduced myself and the whole family. I ran up to where you were... do you remember... I said, 'Hello... I am Margaret Saunders, the eavesdropper, sister of Adrienne and Guy Saunders, daughter of Stephanie Sheila Saunders and Charles Armenius Saunders, niece of Eileen Henrietta Gomez...' Let me tell you, Aunt Eileen hates the name Henrietta... doesn't tell anyone, the same way she doesn't tell anyone her age. Granny Irma says those are the only two matters she knows of on which Aunt Eileen keeps quiet...Where was I... Oh yes... 'niece of Eileen Henrietta Gomez, once married to the late Stephen Herman Gomez, grandniece of Irma Augusta Chase once married to the late Frank William Chase, and also grandniece of the late Iris Ethel Robertson, the late Stanley Ian Robertson... Christopher Michael Robertson now residing in America... and Percival Matthew Robertson also residing in America, granddaughter of Kathleen Maud Harriot and the late John Albert Harriot, great granddaughter of the late Albert Fred Robertson and Hope Amelia Robertson, great great granddaughter of the faded-out Robert Gerald Hinckson and Cecilia Margaret Hinckson... and you are?' But you never answered... I waited but you never replied... instead you just tilted your head and looked at me dressed in all your finery... and Granny Irma who happened to come into the room just as I asked you who you were said, 'Her name is Arabella'. You were not as suprised as I thought you would be when I introduced myself but I knew you understood even though you said nothing... but I must say I was taken by surprise. You stood out so, dressed-up in all your finery... Well, it's only because I wanted you to know something about us, the habits and ways of this household as I've told you before... Adrienne says I have a habit of repeating myself, but it's just to help you understand what you've been thrown into after being hushed up... As I told you before... at least I think I did... I have one brother Guy... he's seventeen... the same age as my cousin Norma... and one sister Adrienne, who's fifteen... they're very much into parties and having girlfriends and boyfriends. Guy is also very serious about his school work... he does it all for her... my mother that is... He knows it pleases her... Not Adrienne... she banks on her beauty... she also goes her own way... Boys like her... she's always getting a message from some boy who likes her... Then there's my father Charles Saunders, who now lives in America. My mother is torn apart by his departure even though she doesn't say it, but I know... we all know... but no one brings it up. The whole thing left her ragged, Granny Irma says... My mother keeps very much to herself as you may have noticed, goes to work and then comes home, kicks off her shoes and falls into bed... She hates wearing shoes... Sometimes she reads a book... sometimes she calls her friend Phyllis Jones to get a good laugh she says... She calls her and laughs... and laughs... and laughs... until she cries... She's changed a lot, was a lot more outgoing, used to entertain a lot... not anymore... Aunt Eileen told Granny Irma that my mother is beginning to let herself go, that a woman should always be careful not to let herself go, and she will make sure it doesn't happen to her... One thing's for certain though... my mother's not happy... Aunt Eileen... you must have heard... her voice carries, Granny Irma says, so even the neighbours can hear if they put their ears to the wall... helps me at least... She's my mother's sister. Norma is her daughter. I don't like Norma very much... only sometimes... She thinks she's above a person like me... as if I care. Granny Irma says Aunt Eileen is bringing her up with the same pretentious ideas she has and those ideas will get her nowhere... pretending to be what she's not, that's what Granny Irma says... Well, of course, you know my Granny Irma Chase... she's really my great-aunt but we all call her Granny Irma... She had you brought here. She's Grandmother's sister, whose house you're living at now... You were sent without choice to Kathleen Harriot's house, Arabella, not that you ever told me this but I know... I feel it in my bones... Want to see something, Arabella?

I'm going to stand on my toes like a ballerina... Look... I almost did it... Look... look... didn't I? Wait until I show Adrienne, she'll be quite surprised... They all think I'm clumsy. The dance teacher Miss Dowding called my mother and said, 'Oh Mrs. Saunders, Adrienne is so very graceful, but Margaret... she's so clumsy...' Looks at me as if to say, 'What is this fool telling me' ... So I no longer go to dancing classes, Arabella... as if I care... Did I tell you about Gladys Davis? No, I don't think I did... I may have mentioned her... no I don't think so... anyway she's Grandmother's very good friend. I'm only mentioning her as she's very close to Grandmother. Granny Irma says she can't stand her... that those thin ankles she has show how mean she is. She says she doesn't understand how Grandmother can be close to such a woman... but then she says the two are alike... they both like money. Anyway, Grandmother relies a lot on Gladys Davis... says that she's truly a friend. Aunt Eileen thinks Gladys Davis is one of the most unattractive women she has ever come across, if not plain ugly. Grandmother says this family is too much into looks and that was the trouble in the first place... Where has looks gotten any of us she asks, but Granny Irma says she will have to settle for the looks... As you can see, it's quite complicated, Arabella. I don't know how many times I've told you all of this, but the more you hear it the better prepared you'll be... Be prepared is my motto... just as Granny Irma says she's prepared for the coming of Christ. Granny Irma says she's on the watch for Christ because he can come at any moment... When we will least expect it he will burst out from the skies like a clap of thunder, Arabella, a flash of light and then a clap... At first we'll all think it's only a thunderstorm, at first we'll be fooled... Oh yes, Christ will arrive with a big bang according to what Granny Irma says... She doesn't actually say big bang but it has to be... and only those who are prepared for that flash and thunderous clap and big bang will be saved... The unprepared will be gobbled up by hellfire... Parched tongues of flame will gobble them up, seeing we're made of more water than anything else... that's what I read. We're just plenty plenty water for those parched tongues... The devil keeps promising those little devils all that water or I think they would desert him... 'Get them on our side,' he says 'and that will be so much more water for you. Fool them and they will lap it all up and then you can lap them all up.'

That's what the devil says... They will lap us up just like our dog laps up the rice Rose gives him. Guy calls him a rice eater, says he's nothing but a rice eater... They must be quite anxious for the end of the world, just as Granny Irma is come to think of it... considering how thirsty they are for us down there... Oh we'd better be on the watch... So you see why you need this information, don't you, Arabella? I may repeat myself, but in the end it will help you... Oh, another thing which I should not forget to mention... even though Granny Irma and Grandmother are sisters, they don't get along very well. I heard Granny Irma say that my grandmother took the house that rightfully belongs to everyone in this family, seeing it came from their mother and her parents, the ones who just faded-out... My grandmother and my now-dead grandfather, Granny Irma says, took the house piece by piece and brought it here and made it their very own only because they had the means to do so... She says my grandmother is into money and property and business like my now-dead grandfather was... that they were two of a kind...

Would you believe, even though I was born here I feel I'm just as much a stranger as you are, Arabella... only gradually came to realise that, so it must be even more difficult for you, but at least you have me to help... Now I had to pick up most of this information by myself... picked it up in a most underhanded way. Do you know I would lie under the bed for hours just to hear something... You're lucky in this respect... you have me to pass on the information... I had no one... have to depend on scoops... Aunt Eileen says you're straight from the bush where Granny

Irma went armed with her Bible to work with the buck people... Don't look like that when I say it... I know how you must feel but I think you're beautiful. I remember when I first saw you I felt I had never seen anything so beautiful. You have added so many colours to my life. I'm only telling you this, as hard as it may seem, so you can understand what you've been thrust into. However, when she said it, Granny Irma curved her mouth downwards and said how dare Aunt Eileen call anyone buck, at least not in front of her and who does she think she is... Miss Hoity-Toity with nothing to show for it... that who she calls buck is the Amerindian who lived in this country even before the white or Black or Chinese or Portuguese or East Indian and they have more right to be here than anyone of us... Well that didn't help much. Aunt Eileen shouted back that Granny Irma is partial to the bucks because she worked with them as a missionary when she got saved and joined the clap-hand church and nothing good ever came out of that either. Just imagine, getting saved by some little American preacher coming here and preaching about hell and damnation and why didn't he preach it to his own people because he knew they wouldn't take him seriously that's why... that only the simple people from this unnamed country would listen to all that rubbish and imagine Granny Irma walking up in public and declaring in public her sins and allowing herself to be dipped in water and rolling on the ground like any common market woman claiming to speak in tongues of fire. It was a disgrace to the family that Granny Irma could join such a Church, that she would even think of leaving the Methodist Church, a loyalty which she at least owed to her parents and their parents, seeing they had all been brought up in that faith, exchanging it for this little clap-hand back alley church. But Granny Irma claims she has been saved and is no longer of this world, whatever that means. She says Aunt Eileen shouldn't talk about any Church Methodist or otherwise since she hasn't stepped into one for how many years, putting aside the occasional wedding and funeral, but she, Irma Augusta Chase, was proud to say that she had removed herself from the Methodist Church where she had paid only lip service for all of those years until Christ entered into her life, that Aunt Eileen needed to look at her life, that no one can live without God in their lives... that everyone needed God whether a King or beggar... and why my mother ever allowed me to join that Roman Catholic Church because I said I had a wish for apparitions and a liking for rosary beads and statues and having my forehead marked on Ash Wednesday was beyond her comprehension, and she would always speak out against it as long as there was still breath left in her old body. Aunt Eileen stamped out of the room saying that she found it hard to answer such ignorance, that Granny Irma was allowing herself to become just as ignorant as *those* people. 'What people?' Granny Irma called after her, 'What people and who did she think she was?'

Can you catch lizards, Arabella? I have a feeling you can. I have a feeling you are even better than me at catching lizards, but you just haven't been given the chance since you came here. Look, I'm going to show you something. I'm going to hook a lizard's head. Let's wait for one to come. Shh, there's one... caught it... Look at how it wriggles. I'm going to spin it round and round. Give it eye-turn. Look how it's spinning. I'm going to spin it to death. Now I bet you can't do that one. You may be able to catch lizards, but can you spin them to death, can you, Arabella?

CHAPTER SIX

At the crack of dawn in a place called Brooklyn, my father was shot by a jealous or angry or hate-filled woman in a bar. My mother doesn't want us to know the details; it's all shush shush, Margaret, like it never took place, just because I asked her... That's the problem with my mother, she hardly says anything... Now if she told us more it might help her and us and it would also save me a lot of trouble, for then I wouldn't have to snoop around the way I do, trying to pick up the crumbs of their conversations. The crumbs only whet the appetite, I would like to tell you. Anyway, I got what I could from the newspapers and what I could pick up around the house. It was right on the front page of the newspaper. Eminent Lawyer Charles A. Saunders killed in Brooklyn... He was in a bar with a woman, that's for certain... Another woman he had been seeing, and who apparently had taken him at face value, like all of them did, like my mother did, Aunt Eileen said, got wind of it and in a burst of rage or hate or jealousy she decided to take a crack at it, so she took her husband's gun which was wrapped up in his trousers in the chest of drawers and blew my father's brains out... According to the newspapers, the woman who was with him said it all happened in a split second... 'His wife knew nothing of the women,' Aunt Eileen said to whoever was in earshot... that she heard this from the horse's mouth itself... She also heard from another very reliable source that his wife is broken up about the whole affair and also the affairs she had had no suspicion of, seeing America is such a big place, not like here where you can't sneeze without somebody saying bless you, no matter where you sneeze... It could be on the road or in a bus or anywhere and invariably a voice will say bless you, which she finds most annoying... She says that human beings will always amaze her, for why should Betty Sharp, of all people, be broken up when she was the prime cause of my mother's and father's split up... but she didn't think of that at the time, did she, and what could she expect? Does a man ever change? Why do women fool themselves that they can do that job? It served her right... What comes around will come around... Stole him from my mother in such a blatant way without shame or regard, now the same thing happened to her but even worse, she pointed out. I may as well tell you from now that once Aunt Eileen gets started it's difficult to put a stop to her. My father's parents left for America for the funeral without even coming to see my mother. Even though they're my grandparents on my father's side, Arabella, we have had very little to do with them. As Grandmother says, they have little background... because of the fêtes they held on the Lord's day... My mother is indifferent, though at first when we were much younger, and she was much happier, she objected strongly to what my grandmother said... but she gradually became indifferent... Now we don't visit them at all. I heard Granny Irma whispering that they will not bring his body back, it will cost too much and that they've taken it very badly...He was their only son, she said, and was treated like a prince from the beginning... They raised enough money from Sunday fêtes to send him away to study, since he was a very bright young man but women were his downfall... couldn't leave them alone... anything in a skirt, Aunt Eileen said... but he was the type of man women fell for... It was his looks that struck, his charm, just the way he had, just a combination of things that you couldn't put into words, but what would make a woman go mad with love like her sister did...

My mother never speaks about it. One day I brought it up and she immediately said people talk too much in this town and I must not get into the habit. My father died and that's it. Granny Irma continued to whisper, not knowing that the walls have ears, that my mother is acting as if nothing has taken place, has not been able to come to terms with very much in her life, Granny Irma says... like his departure or her children... She says it would have been healthier if she had screamed and yelled the way Aunt Eileen can do, the same way Aunt Eileen screamed after her husband was found dead in a bed of roses just as they were about to break into bloom... that it's healthier to get it all out, that she still hasn't gone beyond the point of his departure and has not been able to go anywhere since, that as much as Aunt Eileen's life is a mess, at least she airs it to whoever is within hearing distance...

CHAPTER SEVEN

'Stephanie, I'm worried. At least you might listen to me, you might understand. I know Eileen has no patience with me or what I'm saying... thinks I'm becoming senile... even though she doesn't actually say it, I can see it in her eyes...but you might understand. The cracks... every morning as soon as I wake up I see a new one... every morning. Just suppose they begin spreading all over the house; what are we going to do? This is the only security we have, the only shelter. What are we going to do if this house falls apart? The family is already doing so. Eileen just has enough money from her self-help store to manage with herself and Norma and you don't even have enough for yourself and the children, especially since... since... hmm... Charles' death. At least with the house we don't have an additional burden of rent, so if this falls apart what are we going to do? This house goes back a long time and we have a duty to keep it in the family, if nothing else. Deep cracks over the past weeks just quietly appearing during the night. We need to have a family meeting, talk over things how we plan to manage with everything so uncertain and no men around to help. We need to talk things over...'

'Yes, mummy, I'll speak with Eileen later, but don't worry so much about the house. Things will take care of themselves, they always do. I'll talk with Eileen when I see her.'

'Have you spoken with her yet, Stephanie? I can't remember if you told me.'

'Not yet, mummy, I haven't had the time, but I will. Just stop worrying will you... there is no need to worry.'

CHAPTER EIGHT

'Well it wasn't as if Kathleen wasn't warned,' Gladys Davis said to Mrs. Talbot who happened to be passing by her house. 'Her husband John always told her. Can't lay all the blame on life. I was ther-r-e through it all. I can remember if no one else can. "Kathleen," he used to say in that soft voice he had, too soft for a man I used to think, especially knowing how ha-a-rd he could be when the situation arose. "You're giving Compton too much, you're putting your life on hold for the boy, but he will cause you a lot of pain." But Kathleen never listened or if she did, refused to really hea-r-r. She can be quite ha-a-rd-headed when she sets her mind on something. "Kathleen," he would tell her, "you also have two daughters. You act as if they're not ther-r-e, almost as if they don't exist. It isn't right... you see only him." Not that John did much about it. '

Her daughters Eileen and Stephanie were both very talented girls, you know, Mrs. Talbot, particularly Stephanie. She was quite a gifted child, would race off those math problems like they were nothing. Listening to her play the piano used to be a joy... and how she played when they were first married... played at her own wedding... how happy she was the day they got married... champagne literally flo-o-wed... Her husband Charr-r-les always aimed high, lived high, he liked style as he called it... felt one should live with style... saw himself as a big shot.

They were caught up in each other from the very beginning, I must admit... He did love her, but he was a vain man, couldn't resist the women, needed them to feed his vanity... but he loved her, I still say that... If people had minded their business and not talked so much it might have worked, but they kept her informed... She couldn't help but hear of what would have been better left unsaid... She doesn't play anymore, closed the piano from the time he started with that other woman, Betty Sharp... bare-faced woman already married, but what did she care... the type you know is trouble from the time you set eyes on her... It was a scandal, abandoning husband and four children for him... Oh it was the talk of the town... How she endu-u-red it I don't know... it was ha-a-rd... She suffered... the woman would laugh at her to her face... and Char-r-les just letting it happen... Now with him getting shot it will only make matters worse... Perhaps it would have helped if Stephanie had been given the opportunities Kathleen gave to Compton. At least she would have had something else in her life to hold on to; it could have helped, for without a proper education all she had was the marriage... but the furthering of an education was set aside for the son... I don't think it ever crossed Kathleen's mind to do anything else and John was too wrapped up in his business to interfere. Her daughters would be taken care of by some future husband, but her son would eventually have to look after a family and would also expand their property and business. He would eventually run it all and make a big name for himself and the family... It was always the boy... he was her weak spot... I think he resented her plans for him, was always a sulky child, kept very much to himself, gave the appearance of biding his time, Compton... No, you can't say it happened out of the blue, Mrs. Talbot. Yet when it happened she reacted as if it did... like a cry breaking the silence.'

'Well, she loved him, Mrs. Davis, couldn't help herself, so how much is she to blame?'

'Oh yes, she loved Compton alright but a little too much. Blind to his faults. He lied... he once stole her money. She knew but blamed the gardener... the maid, turning a blind eye to what was going on, what she suspected or perhaps knew but refused to acknowledge... Will never forget that day I received her phone call... "Gladys, Gladys, can you come over please?" The same tone as when John died, that particular tone that is so unlike her that I remember I didn't even ask any questions, just flew over as fast as I could. I remember thinking on my way that someone must have died, for only death could bring on such a tone. Will never forget her face, the distraught look. She handed me a letter, if you can call six lines a letter. *Dea-r-r Aunt Kathleen*, as he always called her, no matter how she insisted she call him mother... *Dea-r-r Aunt Kathleen, I have finally graduated and am now a qualified doctor. I will be getting married to an American girl who also studied medicine. I never wish to see or hea-r-r from you again. You will never see or hea-r-r from me again. Your adopted son, Compton.* I know those words by heart now... not easy to forget them.'

'What you said?'

'What could I say? Could I say, John always told you something like this would happen, that the boy doesn't care for you or anyone but himself... he is only using you? Could I say that, even though I was thinking it? We go back a long time. I couldn't tell her, though she saw it on my face, in my eyes. I'm glad John died before it happened for her sake. Died just before it happened. He would not have said anything either but I remember actually feeling glad that he wasn't alive to see it.'

'She cried?'

'I'm not sure... '

'What you mean? You must know if she cried. You were there.'

'Oh, I know she groaned. I know she made sounds some might call crying. Whatever it was it was terrible to hear. Her brother's son, mother unknown, father gone, brought to her during the rainy season so that the woman had to call out from the gate because the water was too high and she couldn't get into the yard. Holding a bundle calling out, "Miss Harriot... Miss Harriot... a have sumting fuh you"... and Kathleen calling out to Mr. Carlton to put together pieces of wood so that the woman could cross over. "Here," the unknown woman said when she got to the top of the stairs, "is for you, a woman from the village say to give dhis to you. Is Stan child and she don't want it, have enough troubles widout dhis one..." '

'You mean, Mrs. Davis, they never see that woman again?'

'Believe me, never. She left the way she came, never to to be seen again. The baby was quite ill after his arrival, seeing he had come through all that rain for many miles, so he could not even be christened at the time.'

'What a story!'

'Kathleen nursed him for three weeks... never slept... would not allow John or Rose or anyone for that matter to help her. Neglected her husband, her daughters, her house, obsessed by this baby. If anyone brought Compton back to life it's her, Kathleen literally brought him back from the dead and from then could not let him go. If Compton owes anything to anyone he owes his life to her... but the wheel turns, Mrs. Talbot. I have seen it too often in life. He will pay for it. John was always afraid for her after that, never said why and she never helped... shut up herself like a closed book on that point but what could John do? So it was to be... '

... That's what Gladys Davis said to Mrs. Talbot. I went to her house to spend the day soon after my father was shot and that's how I heard her talking about my grandmother. Mrs. Talbot took it all in... Said she had heard rumours but never suspected all of that. She said her husband always reminds her of the old saying whenever she starts to complain about life in general: 'Every time you think you have a bag of troubles,' he tells her, 'take a peek into someone else's bag and then you just going to grab yours and run as fast as you can before someone else grab your bag... Well in this case she will grab her bag as fast as she can and run.'

They didn't know I was under the dining table listening to every word. They never suspected. You see how lucky you are to have me, Arabella. What would you do without me? What?

CHAPTER NINE

My mother has just left the room. She was quite irritated with me, says I have become very secretive. That I was once a very open child but lately I have taken on a very secretive attitude. I don't tell her things any more. I'm not sure what things she means. Anyway, that's what she said. Not a bit like Guy and Adrienne... they talk with her, particularly Guy. He tells her things, I know that. Things she seems very pleased with. Like his coming first every year at school and studying so hard. I heard her say one day to Aunt Eileen that he makes up for much of what she's been through.

Now she calls me secretive, but she has never told me what she's been through. For instance, I didn't tell her about the story I wrote which my teacher was very pleased with. My mother only found out by chance through her friend. She said she felt very embarrassed, almost stupid, standing there and not knowing what Mrs. Rodway was speaking about. 'What was there to hide?' she asked me. Why couldn't she see what I had written? I'll tell you why... I don't mind. Not because I like talking about it. Granny Irma's always telling me to watch my mouth as it'll get me into trouble one of these days. Well, anyway, in case you haven't noticed, in the six months and two days you've been here, Arabella – you see I'm still counting – six months and two days you came out of the bush to stay here, six months and two days and you still haven't said a word. Granny Irma says you can speak, that I'm not to take you at face value. She says if I spend enough time with you you will learn but I need patience and time. Anyway, I'm sure you've noticed by now that this is a house full of secrets, what with all I've been telling you. Rose said as usual that I'm too fast, and I'm going to get in trouble because of that fastness. That I'm into everyting going on in this house. She put her hands on her hips like this and told me just that. Do you know, Arabella, I pretend to be asleep but I'm really wide awake listening. I press as flat as I can against walls to hear what they're saying, whispering behind closed doors... buzz buzz... Sometimes can't tell the difference between a bee and the sound. It starts in the morning with Grandmother's prayers and continues through the day. Always closed doors and she claims I'm secretive... As you know, the only one who talks aloud is Aunt Eileen. I have even started picking up the other telephone so I can hear their conversations. I sometimes tell Adrienne little bits here and there... She thinks it's quite low but she listens to me anyway... and she also hides things. Like the letter she hid in that small chest she has which she always keeps locked. I've tried a few times to open it but it didn't work... I'll find a way though... These things take time. The letter was from my friend's brother. Adrienne actually told me. She doesn't tell me much. I think she has more to say to her friends. She says everything I know comes from books... it's all book knowledge, that I talk as if I know so much when it's all coming from books. I heard her telling one of her friends that *imagine*, I have never ever kissed a boy. Her friend couldn't believe it, told Adrienne they should find a boy for me to kiss. Well they did find one... He told Adrienne's friend that he liked me so they brought him to the house... His name is Phillip Cameron. I sat on the steps with him. He just smiled... I didn't know what to do... was I to kiss him? I could see Adrienne and her friend were watching behind the door. Then he left, said goodbye and left, but what was I to do, Arabella, what was I to do? And I didn't like him anyway. I told her so. Adrienne didn't say anything but I think she was disappointed... Anyway she hid the rose her boyfriend gave her... it's dried up now and I can't understand what she'd want to keep it for when it's all dried up. She also tells my mother she's going to study with her friend Maureen when in fact she's going to meet him. I found his name scribbled in her history book: Lance loves Adrienne, Adrienne loves Lance and a heart drawn next to it. Secretive? Talk about secretive?

What about my father... tell me?

Do you know, Arabella, my mother never told me about my father, my own father, that he was leaving for good? Were you told you would be sent into town, to Kathleen Harriot's house, a place you never knew or dreamt of, not in your wildest dreams? Did they tell you or were you just sent without much notice?

Anyway, she never told me until the very day of his departure and only because I asked her, only because I happened to come into the house for a glass of water at that very moment, or perhaps I would have thought he had just disappeared... poof... gone just like that. We were playing cricket at the back of the Bone's house. I'm the best amongst the girls as you may have noticed. The very best. Not the best at my school work, in fact my mother doesn't hold out much hope for me when it comes to my school work. It's a pity as I think it would please her. I heard her telling Grandmother that I'm not very bright and she was very surprised when I passed the Common Entrance exam. 'Why you've passed, Margaret, you've passed!' she said. Granny Irma thinks I'm a late developer... she says to give me time and I may yet surprise everybody.

'We'll take Margaret... You can have Adrienne, Marilyn, Christine and Carol.' You see, they never make any runs, can't even hold a bat properly and always run off when it's their turn to field. Not me. Have you ever seen me hit one of their balls Arabella? I can hit quite well. That day I went in for the glass of water I had made fifteen runs. That's considered very good for a girl... so there I am quite pleased with my score and just about to go to the fridge when I see her at the window just standing there looking out, you know, fixed, with her chin dropped onto her chest like it always is. So I ran up to her and it was then I saw him, my own father, with Uncle Stanley. They were just about to put his suitcase into the trunk of the car. The wind was strong because my father had to brush his hair away from his eyes as it kept getting in the way. He had long hair, Arabella. He was tall and very handsome, just like Guy is going to be, Granny Irma says...

'Where's Daddy going?' I asked.
'He's leaving,' she replied.
'Leaving?' I asked.
'Yes,' she replied.
'Where to?' I asked.
'America,' she replied.
'When's he coming back?' I asked.
'He isn't coming back,' she replied.

At least I found out then he wasn't coming back, that he was leaving for good, so when I heard he was shot by a jealous woman or an angry woman or a woman too much in love or too much in hate in some place called Brooklyn, Arabella, at least I was a little more prepared. Can you imagine if I hadn't known anything how bad it would have been? At least I knew he was gone for good, so that's no different to being dead is it? It's not as if he ever wrote me or explained anything either. At least I knew he was gone for good, forever, so when I heard he was shot by a woman in some place called Brooklyn, that I only know of from the movies, at least it wasn't as bad as it might have been, at least I was a little prepared.

But since then, since then, I listen, I watch, I investigate even more than I've ever done... like my grandmother does since she discovered the first crack. But she does it only at nights. She walks for hours through the house at nights with her nightgown flared out behind her... There she goes peering and looking and scratching... just like this... I'll show you... she bends her back... See how I'm doing it? Then she pushes her head forward like this so that her body looks just like the bow on Granny Irma's wall that she brought back from the bush. Then she scratches the wall sometimes... schhhhhhhhh... just like that... I don't know why she scratches the wall... Anyway she does... See how I'm doing it? Aunt Eileen calls her the night stalker... it's a movie she saw... Anyway, Grandmother listens, and watches, and stalks, and scratches... says she's trying to find the culprit, that cracks don't just appear out of the blue, there must be a culprit behind it.

I think I'm going to be a detective when I grow up. I have the knack, as my Aunt Eileen says. I have become quite good. I can understand their whispers. At first they were just sounds, hisses, now I can pick up the little bits and pieces they leave scattered here or there and put them together... at least some of it... It can be quite painstaking at times.

They'll not take me by surprise any more, Arabella, no way. I will not take to my bed or room from the shock of it. I couldn't even finish the cricket match that day. Ran off like my sister and her friends. Oh, there's so much going on here and if I didn't try to find out I would be left in the dark like Grandmother and I don't like being left in the dark, do you? Who does? Not me...

That's why I also like books. You can discover many things in books, things you never ever suspected... scoops, plain scoops... like I never ever suspected that the Aztecs used to cut out their victims' hearts to offer as sacrifices to the sun to make sure that it would rise again, to make sure that the sun would defeat that monster of a devil... They would tear their hearts out because they were so afraid... We must fight the devil, my Form

Mistress Mother Carmelita says. We must have backbone and not be like jellyfish so we can fight that devil... I guess even if it means tearing hearts out... I bet you never ever knew that, did you, Arabella? Well if it weren't for that particular book I wouldn't know. When I first read it, I must say my blood ran cold... but then I became accustomed to it. Read it again. The second time I wasn't as afraid but if I told them they would be. Now I'm telling you, Arabella, to prepare you for the next time. So you see why books are important, don't you?

CHAPTER TEN

'If anything ever happens to your mother I don't know what you children will do... if anything ever happens... with your father dead... and I no longer have the means or the strength... with all of that... And then the one thing we could have depended on is now breaking-up before my very eyes and no one is believing me, not Irma, not Stephanie, not Eileen... no one... I am an old woman with not many years left... I just don't know... '

'I dreamt last night that my mother died. I woke up very frightened. It was so unexpected, Arabella.'

'I love you, Margaret,' my mother whispers in my ear so that it tickles and I pull away. 'I love you very much.'

'If Mummy asks where you got those books, Margaret, tell her you had them a long time... Don't let her know I just bought them for you.' She hides things from Grandmother when she buys so that she won't see how much she spends, seeing she has to keep borrowing from her to pay our school fees and helping her out in general.

'Is that a new dress, Margaret?'

'No, Grandmother, I've had it a long time.'

'You children will never understand the sacrifices I've made for you... what I have given up for you... what I have been through for you... you will never understand,' my mother said to me while we were lying down together on Granny Irma's bed.

What does she mean, Arabella? It isn't the first time she's said it, that's the problem with my mother... She doesn't talk... doesn't explain things... If she did it would help me... then I wouldn't have to snoop around the way I do trying to pick up the crumbs of their conversations.

CHAPTER ELEVEN

Rose ran through the gate shouting at the top of her voice.

'Dhey burnin' it dung, dhey burnin' it dung!'

'What, what are they burning down? Calm yourself. Who's they? Speak clearly,' Granny Irma asked.

'Dhe people burnin' dhe tung dung. Dhe people gone mad. If yuh see dhem wid pointer brooms wavin' in dhe air right and left bawlin' out, sweep dhe British away, sweep dhem away. A frighten when a firs' see dhem movin' dung dhe streets. Is a sight to behold.'

'Are we going to burn up? Are we going to burn up?' I asked.

'Don' axe me, chile, I don' know anyting anymore. Everyting crazy... like hell break loose,' replied Rose.

Mr. Carlton ran through the gate shouting at the top of his voice too.

'Dhey lootin' all dhe stores, takin' everyting dhey can lay dhere hands on. Plenty plenty people carryin' plenty plenty tings on dhere backs, on dhere bicycles, on dhere donkey carts, on dhere trucks, on dhe tops a cars, on anyting dhey can lay dhere hands on. New bicycles, new stoves, new carpets, new shoes, new suits, new record players, new furniture, new transistors, new watches, dhey just takin' whatever dhey can lay dhere hands on. Is pure madness out dhere, Miss Harriot, pure madness.'

'Eileen's store burn down,' Gladys Davis called and told my grandmother.

'Eileen's store burn down,' my grandmother told Granny Irma.

'Eileen's store burn down,' Granny Irma told my mother.

'Aunt Eileen's store burn down,' my mother told my brother.

'Aunt Eileen's store burn down,' my brother told my sister.

'Aunt Eileen's store burn down,' my sister told me.

'What is she going to do?' we all chorused.

'What is she going to do?' Granny Irma asked. 'Who would believe it?' she asked. 'Who would believe it? If you had told me Eileen would be where she is now a few years back I would not have believed it. I would have said you were crazy. As much as I know about the ups and downs of this life, I still would not have believed it.'

'It was one of the weddings of the year when she married Stephen Gomez... I must say he was a handsome man who was of Portuguese descent... many of the women were after him. I must say he was a dashing fellow with a succcssful future laid out for him... ready made... had no hand in it... Perhaps that was the trouble... not much brains, but who needs it in this country to make money... in fact brains could be your downfall... Between his colour and the money his father had, and the strings he could pull, with all of that going for him, he didn't need much more. Could pick up any job just like that... through a phone call.

'I must say they made a handsome couple. Your aunt had beautiful skin at the time but troubles have added a few lines here and there as things haven't gone as expected. If you children had seen her in her youth, this beautiful coloured girl with a man of Portuguese descent with a future laid out which he had no hand in. But that's all he had... looks and colour. Otherwise was a wastrel. Drank so much he couldn't hold down a job for any length of time. If it weren't for that self-help store she opened where she sold pastries, cakes and local craft mainly to the white people – for who else could afford those extra frills? – I don't know how they would have managed, especially after she had Norma. Then he finally got a job and seemed to be holding it down, when poof, out of the blue there he is in the garden she had laid out, worked on from the first day of their marriage; there he was inhaling the perfumes, as he called it, when he fell down dead as a door nail on her beautiful bed of roses, just as they were breaking into bloom. Would you believe it? Who would believe that is where the whole thing would end, on a bed of roses.

It was the neighbour who saw. Said she happened to be looking out of the window when she saw him fall forward... just like that. At first she said she thought he had slipped because the ground was soggy with all the rain we were having at the time, or that the scent was too strong for him, but then she realised he wasn't getting up. Ran over and called out, 'Mrs. Gomez, Mrs. Gomez, your husband fell down on the bed of roses.' He was already dead, dead as a door nail by the time Eileen got to him. Took ages to get him out of that tangle; the thorns would not let go... Now what is she going to do?'

Aunt Eileen just stood there biding her time and then yelled at Granny Irma that she is the last one to talk about her life, that at least her husband left her with a little insurance money, though not much to talk of, at least it was able to carry her for a year and she was one to talk about her marrying a man only because of his colour when hadn't she done the same and at least she got a daughter out of the marriage and money to carry her for a year while Granny Irma got nothing except an ulcer and a pair of scissors, that was all, for hadn't Granny Irma's husband returned from work one day, never to return, but instead chose to sit in a chair in the drawing room and smoke his pipe, and hadn't Granny Irma nagged him and nagged him to get up stand up and work like a man should, but he never moved, never bothered to reply to her but continued to sit and ponder and look out of the window and smoke his pipe... the very pipe that would kill him, even after the doctors had told him that if he continued to smoke he would die. Didn't he pace the floor for two hours and twenty minutes, for didn't Granny Irma time him, and then returned to his chair and relit his pipe and died just as the doctors had predicted, for it was Granny Irma herself who had informed us of the matter. And imagine, after taking all of that, what did she get for it but an ulcer and a pair of scissors.

Granny Irma then yelled back that admittedly it was true that she, Irma Augusta Chase, was willed one pair of scissors by her now-deceased husband, Frank William Chase, but hadn't she cut her losses and with that same pair of scissors turned to dressmaking so that she would eventually become one of the best dressmakers in the town, if not the best. While what did Aunt Eileen do with her money but spend it on clothes, keeping up the same pretensive life style that from the beginning had got her nowhere and would continue to get her nowhere and now the money had dwindled to a pittance. But had she used it on anything productive? Oh no, she was too great for that but at least she, Irma Augusta Chase, had cut her losses and turned to dressmaking and from that same pair of scissors was able to support herself until this very day, without having to pretend to be what she was not, and will be able to support herself to the end through the grace of Our Lord Jesus Christ who through his mercy had saved her from hell itself and at least she had enough put aside to cover the cost of her burial... Could Aunt Eileen say that, could she?

They were both out of breath when it was all over. Granny Irma had to take a glass of water to get over that rude woman who had no respect for her grey hairs... and, now that she had the chance to mention it... for why shouldn't she kill two birds with one stone...? Why shouldn't she...? For how many opportunities did a person get to kill two birds with one stone...? She has noticed over the past months that Aunt Eileen now calls her by her first name, picking up the style of her so-called jetset friends. Aunt Eileen downed a rum and water to relax her nerves.

CHAPTER TWELVE

Arabella, listen. I've something very very special to tell you, something only you would understand and perhaps Rose... yes, perhaps? You have to promise on your word of honour you wouldn't tell anyone the day you start talking, okay? How should I say it, how shall I start? Hmmm... I'll just whisper it as the walls have ears... I have a baku... well? Rose and Mr. Carlton first gave me the idea.

You see one day I happened to tell Rose about my mother, the sacrifices she is making for us and how afraid I am that something might happen to her especially since my father was shot. Now I'm even more afraid since reading about the Aztecs and their sacrifices. 'What does she really mean,' I asked Rose, 'when she says that she is sacrificing herself for us?' Well, Rose wanted to know who told me my father was shot. That I musn't listen so much to what other people say, that my father is dead but it was just an accident. She also said I read too much. But at least she listened, she always does. That's what I like about her... she listens. Then I told her about my dream... that my mother was laid out in a coffin on the back of a donkey in the same bush you came out of, Arabella. I just knew it was the place you came from as soon as I saw it... but it was quite dark. And then, as luck would have it, the very next day I heard Rose talking to Mr. Carlton about Dr. Sharpton's baku. Dr. Sharpton is a Portuguese man who is very well off, Aunt Eileen says, not like this family. She says when it comes to money Dr. Sharpton doesn't have anything to bother him, not like this family. Rose told Mr. Carlton that ever since he got his baku he has just been making plenty plenty money and having plenty plenty luck. She said that the baku lives in a saucepan in the tree in front of Dr. Sharpton's house and that she Rose Elmfield has seen the baku with her own two eyes. She said quite a few people have heard him banging away on the saucepan. She said a friend of hers jumped out of her skin one night when she was going home, for just as she stepped under the tree the banging started... Apparently her friend fled...

Well, anyway, I thought of her, you know, her, my mother. So I asked Rose after Mr. Carlton left what a baku was. 'Yuh like to lis'en too much,' she said. 'Always lis'enin' to everyting.' She waited a little before she told me that a baku is a little short man.

'As short as Mr. Wood?' I asked.

'No much shorter. About eight inches.'

'That small? Where does he come from?'

'A fowl egg,' said Rose.

'A fowl egg?'

'Yes. A frog lay on dhe fowl egg and dhe baku hatch. But you have to be careful wid him. You have to feed him wid banana and milk. He could bring you plenty plenty luck but if you make him angry he could cause plenty plenty bad luck.'

I didn't tell you all of this before, Arabella... Anyway, now you know. He lives under the house. I offered to have him live in the ginnip tree in a saucepan since Dr. Sharpton's baku lives in a tree in a saucepan but he said that just because Dr. Sharpton's baku lives in a tree in a saucepan it doesn't mean every baku wants to do the same, that if someone lived in a hut does it mean I would like to live in a hut. So he finally settled for the storeroom under the backsteps.

Well, another reason I'm now telling you all of this is

because I'm a bit worried. I've already told you about the cracks my grandmother claims she's seeing and now she thinks her house is falling apart before her very eyes, breaking up and no one else is believing her, no one seeing the cracks. Is she mad or something? 'How can cracks just appear?' she complains, and I have to admit this only started after the baku arrived. I must be very careful with him. He's strange. His head looks like a tiny dried-up mango seed just as if someone sucked all the juice out of it, but then what can you expect, Arabella, think of it... a frog lay on a fowl egg and he hatched...

He never allows me to touch him. I can talk to him he says but never ever touch him. I think it's because he's so small and I could make mincemeat of him. He's quite shrewd. He has to be, I guess, don't you think so? His brains would definitely have to make up for his size or he would be a goner. He never ever gets too close to me. Whenever I go to see him he draws a distinct line with a mud ball he has... he wets it and then draws the line. He warns me that I must never ever go beyond that line... never...

I've told him all about you, Arabella, and how you weren't even told that you'd have to leave the bush, that you were just taken and brought here and from the shock of it we can't get a screech out of you since the day you arrived. I told him you're also grieving, so he knows about you. I have to treat him very well, feed him very well, but I did it because of her, my mother, only to help her to prevent her from being sacrificed... I read about the Aztecs and I became afraid for her when she said she was sacrificing herself for us. So when I heard Rose and Mr. Carlton that day I felt I could help her.

Wouldn't you be afraid if you also read that people once tore out their victims' hearts, their very hearts, right here, Arabella? I can hear my heart... boop boop boop... boopboop... let me feel yours. Why, it's fluttering... Oh you must be very afraid for it to flutter like that. Don't worry, the baku won't hurt you, at least

I don't think so...

Well anyway, the Aztecs removed that sound, they tore the sound out, pulled those bleeding hearts out as a sacrifice to the sun so that it could beat up that monster of a devil and rise again, with the blood dribbling down their wrists and elbows like cherry juice... That's some of what the book said and some is what I think... heart-pumps pumping their blood-juice out, making it surge onto their faces and into their mouths. Their hearts would begin to cough and cough... gugh gugh, like that... and all that blood-juice would be hawked up and surge onto their faces and into their mouths giving them a taste for blood... making them blood-thirsty...The book didn't say that, Arabella, I'm saying it. Whenever the Aztecs fought a war they would capture their enemies and keep them locked away until the time came for the sacrifice... It was like a big festival I think... there were so many captured enemies waiting that the sound of their beating hearts could be heard from quite a distance... bippety bop, bippety bop... Some beat fast, some beat slow, some just went at the normal rhythm, some fluttered like yours, so you had to press your ears against their chests to hear them... the bigger the heart, the louder it went... hearts and hearts and hearts drumming with fear or ecstasy or excitement or... whatever... Anyway, the people and the priests would hear the sound and at first they would start tapping their fingers, then the next thing you knew they were tapping their feet, and the next thing you knew they left whatever they were doing, because at this point they couldn't help themselves and they would begin dancing and whirling round and round and round in the streets to the hypnotic beat of the beating hearts and, as the time drew closer to the big day, the prisoners' hearts would begin to hammer against their chests, so by the time the day of the sacrifice arrived everyone, Arabella, everyone, priests and people and the prisoners to be sacrificed, would be in a frenzy running amok.

Do you know I mentioned this to Mother Carmelita at school and she put me in detention and told me I am not to read those books. Does my mother know I am reading such dangerous books? I only told her because you hadn't arrived as yet and I didn't have anyone to talk to, at least not with what I have to say and Rose was away for two weeks... Her husband had come to see her... She hadn't seen him in a long time, so she took two weeks off, so then I had no one to tell. She was quite pleased when her husband came but she came back sad... at least I think so... I asked her anyway and she told me that sometimes I can be quite kind. She said he had decided to go back to look for the gold which she thinks he will never find... So out of sheer desperation to tell someone I decided to tell Mother Carmelita. I thought she would understand since Christ also laid himself out as a sacrifice and there was also blood and she herself has sacrificed marriage and children and love and money for Christ... She is as dead to the world as Granny Irma is, so I naturally thought she would appreciate my point of view. But she didn't, instead she only became angry. So you can see why I was so afraid... First I dream that my mother died laid out in a coffin on the back of a donkey in the bush where I'm sure you came from, though it was quite dark but I knew it was the place you came from... Then my grandmother, who keeps saying that if anything ever happens to my mother she doesn't know what will happen to us, as if she expects something, as if she is prepared... and now to top it all I go and read about the Aztecs. At least I've heard about Christ... but I thought that was the only sacrifice there ever was... How was I to know it got into our blood so there were plenty plenty plenty more sacrifices? How was I to know there was so much blood? Can you imagine, Arabella, how much blood there must be in the world when you think of how many people there are... gallons and gallons and gallons of blood... Wouldn't you be afraid? I'm sure you would be.

So when I heard Rose and Mr. Carlton I felt very relieved. I wasn't as frightened... not that I stopped praying. But perhaps things would start getting better for my mother if I got a baku, for if it could help Dr. Sharpton, then it could help my mother, that's what I thought. And Dr. Sharpton also goes to church. I see him there every Sunday with his wife and three children... his daughter is in my class... she thinks a lot of herself... that's what my friend Joy says and I agree with her... just because she comes first every year, gets the conduct bow for good behaviour and the gold bow for her school work. Every time we have **Reading of Marks**, her name is read out first...There is Mother Carmelita who sits right next to the Reverend Mother; the Reverend Mother reads out our marks in front of the whole school so we all know where we stand with each other... 'A, Carol Sharpton... A-, Jackie DeCairies, Elizabeth Marks, Donna Hugh...' and on she goes... I'm always hoping that she will read out my name for something, even for trying... Anyway, as I was saying, seeing Dr. Sharpton is always in church and yet still feels he needs a booster like a baku, then I felt it was also okay for me to get a baku too.

And at first things seemed better. My mother seemed a little happier, more relaxed, especially after Guy passed his exams, but then the cracks started. Out of the blue Grandmother woke up one morning and claimed she saw a crack and each morning she claims she sees another one and no one believes or listens... She's now telling my dead grandfather that the cracks are beginning to spill out all kinds of things, just like her mother did two weeks before she died. Aunt Eileen thinks it's because of my grandfather's and Uncle Ralph's death, but my grandfather died many years ago, so why should it start affecting her only now, Arabella? ...And she's been talking to him for all these years as if he's still here... Anyway, Aunt Eileen thinks it's because of them and also Uncle Compton and her age, but we know better don't we, Arabella, we believe her, don't we, because we know anything can happen, don't we... anything... like my father being shot by a woman in a bar? The important thing is not be taken by surprise.

If only the baku would allow me to take you to him, but he keeps saying no, no, no... I notice he's quite determined for his size... no more than eight inches, just enough to fit in a bottle. I told him that one day, I said, 'I could easily fit you into a bottle and close it up.' I don't think he liked what I said, looked a bit pale, didn't reply, but I know him fairly well by now... Perhaps I will take you anyway... take you to see him whether he likes it or not...

CHAPTER THIRTEEN

'You must deal with it,' he said, 'get the family together and deal with it.'

'But aren't you dead, John? You have been dead for all these years. What do you have to do with it?'

'It's falling apart,' he said.

'I know,' she replied.

'Did you see him?' he asked.

'You mean that little man about eight inches tall? The stocky one whose skin reminds me of cornflakes?'

'Yes that one.'

'Did you see him when you were coming up the stairs? He just sat there sunbathing on the stairs as if he were on a beach, sunbathing and absolutely naked like the day he was born. What could I say? I couldn't believe it. Just sitting there sunbathing as if he owned the place as naked as the day he was born.'

'Dhey coming!' Rose cried out. 'Dhey coming, Miss Harriot! Close dhe doors, keep dhem out, close dhe doors.' She can see the faces pressed on the glass pushing to get in.

'You will have to deal with it,' he said.

'The faces, there are too many faces. I don't have the strength,' she replied. 'I am not the same person you left behind when you died. Perhaps you are still back to the time when you died when I was still a strong woman in control of my life and house and money. It's all being wiped out,' she said. 'Everything... everything. All that we worked so hard for... How will I replace it? I am now an old woman and no longer have the energy, the inclination, and you now dead all these years. How can I replace it? Then there is Stephanie... just a shell of her former self, and I am left with the blame... You are dead... '

She sat on the stool and wept. She wept and wept and wept, so that when she awoke she was certain they must have heard her in the house, they must have heard the weeping.

I could hear Grandmother crying from my bedroom. It was quite late at night. Adrienne was fast asleep next to me. She had gone to a party the night before and came in quite late. My mother was quite upset but Adrienne didn't care. My mother saw Lance kissing Adrienne on the verandah and became quite angry, which surprised everyone.

Nothing could ever wake Adrienne my mother says. If the house fell around her she wouldn't know... takes after her, she says... they both sleep like the dead. But I am too much on the alert she feels. The slightest sound and I wake up. Too much on the alert she thinks, while she's just the opposite.

I could hear my grandmother. Couldn't be grieving because then one didn't hear anything except a plopping sound. I know that from experience... So why was she crying? Then it stopped. I could hear her getting up. The bedroom door opened. She dragged along the floor in the dark. Once in a while she would stumble against a piece of furniture but she was obviously now better at it.

In the beginning she would actually fall against the pieces, hit herself against the walls but not anymore. Only if something was inadvertently left in the way would she now stumble against it. She could feel her way in the dark... her eyes had grown accustomed to the dark over the past few weeks. Just like you, Arabella, she would pause for a moment, her head cocked to one side, her eyes darting from side to side, looking, listening, eating it all up. In fact, it is just as if she's beginning to eat up the darkness and this is what helps her to find her way through the house. She's beginning to swallow parts of the darkness.

I heard her and I trembled in the dark. Suppose she came upon the baku... just suppose she did... just suppose...

CHAPTER FOURTEEN

'Your mother isn't looking well, Eileen,' Gladys Davis said after paying a visit to Grandmother. She went down to Aunt Eileen to speak to her because she said she was very concerned. Granny Irma was not at home.

'She looks very tir-r-ed and for the first time is beginning to look her age... is even losing weight,' she told her.

'I know,' Aunt Eileen replied, 'but she is so caught up in this thing that is supposed to be happening in the house. No matter how you tell her it isn't, that it's all in her mind, that it's a result of all that has been happening... my father, Compton, and then Uncle Ralph, she wouldn't listen. Insists that there are cracks and the house is falling apart and what will happen to her with her husband gone. Is she to end up like Ruby? How can she trust us? I keep telling her that whatever happens we will never let her end up in an old people's home, but she doesn't believe. Refuses to believe. Wants to hold a family conference as she calls it.'

'What about Irma? What does she think about the entire matter?'

'Well you know how she's caught up in that back alley church. Any opinion she gives is connected to her salvation. Feels it's the judgement of God. Her sister got too caught up in her property and money, exchanged these things for her very soul and this is the result. Her sister needs salvation, she says, true salvation, not just attending a church every Sunday. Her sister needs to be transformed at her very heart, just as she was... How could she put it into words... the peace that passeth all understanding, how could she convey it, one could only experience it. Says we are all damned and are letting the children be open to all kinds of influences, particularly Margaret whom she feels should be watched more carefully, taken in hand or it will be too late. I don't know why she's telling me that for I say the same thing... But with Irma, when I speak it goes in one ear and comes out the other. Those American missionaries certainly have a hold on her.'

'Yesterday one of them came to visit her and actually had the effrontery to call me sister. I quickly informed her that I am no sister of hers, just to understand that... Sister indeed... She feels it isn't good to leave Margaret the way we do, especially since she reminds her so much of Iris that at moments she has the feeling that Iris has come back to haunt us all. You ever heard such rubbish in all your life? And as I tell her, I have enough on my hands without taking on Margaret... Sometimes I feel like I'm living in a madhouse what with mummy and the imaginary cracks and Irma on being saved... even complaining that I no longer call her Aunt Irma... me... a big woman with a child to still call her Aunt. Believe me, if I had the money I would move out tomorrow with Norma... '

CHAPTER FIFTEEN

'Come, Arabella... I'm going to play a game of litty... Watch where you're going. I keep forgetting you wouldn't know what litty is would you? Look out! Now you almost made me slip... Say it... look out... look out... look out... Say it... Well, anyway, we need eleven small stones... smooth ones... Let's see if we can find them? We'll look in the garden, usually you can find good ones there... See, I told you...Look... I've found seven already... hmmm... Here are two more... Let's see this one? No it's too rough. Arabella, those are perfect. Where did you find them? Would be perfect for a sling shot. Good, you've picked up just the ones I need... I'm better at jacks but I lost the ball... I'll play under the house. You really picked up some nice stones, as if you knew just what I wanted... you never fail to surprise me... To think Aunt Eileen calls you bird-brained... Little does she know... You've seen far more than they can ever imagine in their wildest dreams, but you are just as secretive as I am and I don't blame you. Who can you trust? I mean look how they just took you away and brought you here... Want a piece of mango? Here, take this... My friend Joy Small is going to have a fête at her house. She asked her father and he said it's okay once she cleans up afterwards. She's invited me... I don't particularly like going to fêtes. Adrienne and Guy like fêtes. Adrienne is not a wall-flower, that's why... I heard Aunt Eileen telling Granny

Irma that... Do you know, Arabella, the last fête I went to, Guy promised to dance with me but never did so. I sat all night and no one else cared to do so... My mother asked me if I danced and I told her no and she told Aunt Eileen later... I heard her... She whispered, 'poor Margaret'. Guy says I'm getting too fat, that's why... I know he crashes fêtes... He pretends he's so well behaved, never fails to tip his cap to all and sundry and yet he likes to crash fêtes, would you believe that, Arabella. I heard him telling Adrienne that they threw him out of one last night... he wasn't invited but there was a girl there he wanted to meet... I heard him say that the girl ignored him anyway and then he said, 'fuck it'. Aunt Eileen says it's good he has an outlet because he studies so hard, but if she only knew, if she only knew... but I know and now you know.

Do you remember that baku I told you about? Oh no, I missed that one... am a bit out of practice... remember the baku I said I would take you to if he would allow me? Well there's something I didn't tell you, something I left out because I wasn't quite sure if I could trust you enough. Well now I'm sure. When I first got him I was quite pleased and I think he was also. We were both pleased with each other. I fed him well, never missed giving him his bananas and milk. He even began to put on weight, fill out as my grandmother says. His head no longer looked like a mango seed. It must have been the milk. He loved it, drank my share and Adrienne's without her knowing. It was easy to take her share as she hates it... Not me... I could drink the whole pot. I don't like food but I like milk and chocolates. Granny Irma also says that's why I'm putting on so much weight.

Sometimes I would even give him a little extra. I can't believe you've finished that mango so quickly. Hold on, I'm going to pelt one down from Mr. Bone's tree... he and Mrs. Bone are out... Here's a nice one... try and go a little slowly with this one... Now where was I? At the baku... Aunt Eileen says I should try to stick to what I'm saying and not wander off on something else as I do... She says it's most annoying, that it's time I grow up and stop acting like a ten year old child. Well, as I told you the last time, Arabella, if you remember, there was a definite change in my mother... She looked happier, laughed more, talked more with me, even actually sat down to play a game of jacks with me... Then got a raise in her pay... She began going out again, wearing those beautiful dresses she used to wear when my father was here. I'm sorry you never met him. I think you would have liked him... he was that sort of person... easy to like... too easy, Aunt Eileen says. He would not have called you dumb, that's for certain... neither does my mother... I don't think she really notices you, but if she did she wouldn't call you dumb. Rose likes my mother... Anyway it all started when we went to the country for a month. I hate going there to that old house. I'm always afraid it will come tumbling down while we are asleep. And did you notice how black the nights are without electricity, how very black? It's a different kind of darkness to the one here... Did you notice? I'm sure you did. I'm always afraid at nights. One night I actually saw a ball of fire in the sky. I told Adrienne and she nearly died laughing. She says my head is full of rubbish, but I saw it... it flew right outside the window. It's Rose who told me that old higues go about at nights like balls of fire. She told me that old higues are really very very old women who change into balls of fire at nights... they go about at nights looking for blood... 'How can we stop them?' I asked her. 'How can we?' She said we can slow them down by putting rice at our doors... For some reason they cannot... cannot... pass rice... They just have to stop and count the grains... each grain... that's how they're caught she said... In the morning they're found counting and counting. I can tell you, Arabella, if it weren't for Rose I wouldn't know a thing... Ever since that night I put two plates of rice at the back and front doors to keep the old higue out but of course I didn't let anyone know... they would think I'm crazy... but I'm not taking any chances... not me... She feeds on blood and if she got to know that my mother is laying herself out as a sacrifice, Arabella, can you imagine what would happen? I mean that would be a meal ticket for her, new blood. I mean it must be hard to come by blood since there isn't such a huge supply of hearts. I think she used to sneak over to the Aztecs and suck some of the victims' hearts out. I don't think the Aztecs even noticed, there were so many... but now she has to forage like any other animal... No, I couldn't let her get wind of the fact that my mother is laying herself out... So from that night I keep two plates of rice at the front and back doors. At least I don't have to keep changing them... They're always there the next morning, thank goodness because between finding bananas and milk for the baku and rice for her I would go mad. No, I can't say I like it there very much, especially since seeing that ball of fire.

Anyway we went there as usual to give my mother a break, you know she has us all year, she needs the break. Well I did make sure to leave him some bananas and milk, but that's where I think the trouble started. He doesn't actually say it, he's a person of few words and now those words are mainly curse words... Anyway, when we returned and I went to see him, even I was a bit taken aback at how much weight he'd lost. He looked different, dried up... also the expression in his eyes wasn't the same. That's what frightens me about him, he's constantly changing. I never know what to expect. This time his eyes reminded me of the marbles I have, that's what I said to him as soon as I saw him. 'Your eyes have changed... At first they were hardly noticeable but not anymore,' I said to him. 'They now look just like the marbles I have,' and then and there I decided that marbles are for playing not for seeing. I like marbles but then and there I said I didn't like marble eyes. There was a difference, a definite difference.

Jesus, he was angry! ... If Granny Irma heard me say that she would go crazy... She says, 'You children are not to call the

Lord's name in vain'. First thing he said was, 'You left me here for one month with nothing to eat.' 'That's not true, I did leave you bananas and milk,' I told him, 'and, looking at your size, how was I to know you were that greedy.' But apparently the milk had gone sour the very next day and the bananas only lasted for a week. Said he was quite sick. I had to admit that he looked thinner, more drawn, but I pointed out that he looked just like that when he first came so why should he be so angry. Well, perhaps I should not have said that, but how was I to know, Arabella, how was I to know... just tell me that? Am I psychic? I told him I would have taken him with us but, as short as he is, where could I have hidden him, tell me? He doesn't allow me to touch him in the first place... then would he ever let me put him in a bottle? Oh, no... I told him to be reasonable. I have never had to deal with a baku before, except for the little Rose told me, so what does he expect. Well things got worse. For some reason, Rose stopped buying the bananas and the milkman was ill for a while. 'What am I to do?' I said to him. 'Do you expect me to stick my neck out? Do you expect me to steal? Do you expect me to steal and then suffer from so much guilt that I would end up in hiding like Aunt Iris, acting like any common thief? Is it my fault that there are no bananas or milk in the house? What do you expect me to do? What are you demanding of me in return for a pot of luck for my mother? A pot can hold so much and no more,' I said. I even promised I would get him some mangoes, seeing it was the mango season and mangoes were much sweeter than bananas anyway. I mentioned how much you liked them, Arabella. Well, he stamped his foot and his eyes reminded me of marbles more than ever and he said that if things didn't improve soon, then I would regret it, that things would start happening that I never dreamt of. 'You brought me here,' he said, 'and it's your responsibility to look after me.' 'I'm only a child,' I said to him but he no longer listens. I became so afraid of him I stopped going... maybe I should not have done so, you know what I mean. I thought that if I stopped, perhaps he would go away go to another house where he could be fed... even join Dr. Sharpton's baku... Then the cracks started appearing. That bothers me as much as my mother does, so that's a lot of bother for my age isn't it? Where can they be coming from? Then my grandmother prying into the matter trying to get the culprit. Suppose, just suppose, Arabella, it's him... just suppose... Then she may catch him, and if she does, you can see why I didn't tell you can't you? Well, we'll just have to wait and see won't we?

Arabella, Arabella, guess what? It's much worse than I thought. Remember I said I would go to see him... Well I did. When I saw him I could hardly believe it. He frightened me more than ever the way he looked... He looks much thinner... his head now looks just like a tiny calabash and his eyes seem to bulge out like stuck-on mud balls, even worse than the marbles... At least I was accustomed to that. His eyes are full of mud... he just sat there and never said a word. Then before I could get in a word he started to curse me and each word became a stone and as the words pelted out of his mouth they became stones... a shower of stones falling on me, hitting me... they were flying from his mouth, each word a stone falling hard hard, and as each fell the thinner he got. He started shrinking right before my eyes. Do you see how bruised-up I am? What am I going to do? If only you could talk you might be able to tell me something... you must have picked up a few words considering how much I've been talking to you... Oh, it's much worse than I ever imagined isn't it... isn't it?

CHAPTER SIXTEEN

The old woman knows the child's eyes are focused on her. Lately the child has been following her. She knows it and even when she is alone the eyes leave their trace, leave her with a feeling of being a marked woman, as if the child's very expression were so intense it was able to tattoo itself onto her back. 'Iris... where is that girl?' their mother would ask. 'Find her, Kathleen. I need her to help in the house. Iris, Iris... One can never find her when one needs her. She must also give a hand in the house. Kathleen, go and see where she is and tell her to come home at once.' Their mother seemed to fear Iris, though it was never said aloud, but they could see it, could see the way her eyes would seem to probe Iris's very thoughts as if trying to pick up something. 'Where were you?' she would demand. 'What were you doing... you couldn't only be reading books... It doesn't make sense. Why do you have to sneak off the way you do? Are you hiding? If so from what?' Shaking, shaking Iris, as if in the shaking a few words would drop onto her lap... Their father hitting Iris as if she were one of his own sons with a back strong enough to bear the blows... Stan grabbing the cane out of their father's hands, fighting him for the cane... Iris, who was always seen as the one who could easily be taken advantage of, a walkover... Iris, who pursued the word but hardly uttered one, hiding like any common criminal, it was said, reminding you of their mother who would be seen looking furtively over the shoulder or furtively ahead or furtively sideways, as if expecting to come up on something or avoiding something. An accidental bumping into would cause an overdosed reaction, as her husband would say... She had to trail Iris, hunt her, eyes pressed against the earth, trying to pick up a crushed leaf, a page, a written inscription... as she was wont sometimes to bend down and write on the earth... indeed, she would always leave a trace of herself behind so that you would eventually come upon her buried as usual in the leaves of a book.

'It's all coming back, John,' she said. 'The whole thing is raising it's head...That child doesn't help either... There are eyes everywhere... your eyes, Iris's eyes, the child's eyes... none of you will let go. At my age to have to go through this, at my age to feel as if I'm a marked woman. Why me, tell me? You are long dead and gone but you are still part of it. What have I done to deserve this inquisition? Am I any more guilty than you or anyone else for that matter? Are we not all the same in the eyes of God? So why me? Why should I have to go through the guilt ... It isn't fair, not at my age... not at my old age... '

I was hiding behind the door, Arabella, and I heard my grandmother talking to my dead grandfather as she has always done, even though he's been dead all these years she has never stopped talking with him... I know... so when I heard her I asked her, Arabella, I actually asked her if she's seen anything, anything, just to find out, but she said no, but she is beginning to sense something. I asked her, 'What, what are you beginning to sense, Grandmother?' 'Leave me alone, leave me alone!' she shouted. 'Go and meet with friends like any normal child, but leave me alone, stop trailing me as if I am a marked woman... Stop pestering me, following me around... Leave me alone all of you.' But it's because I can't find the baku, Arabella. I crept up very quietly to the storeroom but he wasn't there. At first I expected a shower of stones, the abuse, but there was nothing.

But I know he hasn't left. I know because I could see his clothes; they were folded very neatly right at the entrance. Where can he be? I then decided to leave a note for him telling him that I will be going to see him tomorrow, that it's important I speak to him, perhaps we can come to some sort of agreement. I set the time for 3 pm. I told him that I have bananas and milk to give him. I know just from sheer greed he will meet me. I haven't decided yet what I will say to him but I will have to think about it... If only you would talk, if only you would say something, I know you would help me, wouldn't you, Arabella?

He didn't even have the basic courtesy to turn up would you believe it...

CHAPTER SEVENTEEN

My friend Joy Small told me at school today that her family is leaving. She says her father told her that the communists will take over.

So many girls I know are leaving. They're going to Canada, America or England. They tell me their parents told them that the communists will take over, the communists will take all property away from their owners, children away from their parents, but most terrible, they will take away God. They will handcuff God and take Him away to some very lonely place where no one will ever hear from Him again. They say that's the most terrible thing of all having God taken away, worse even than taking the children would be to take away God. I suggested to Rose that the communists must all be like pied pipers. She said she didn't know what pied pipers were and she didn't care. I told her anyway. I said they must be quite good at the piping of tunes seeing they could lead God away and make Him disappear, but we must have broken our word over something otherwise the pied pipers would not have to take such a course of action. I was not so surprised that they could take children away from their parents as that wouldn't be the first time it happened. It just meant they would play the same old tune that first did it... but the tune that could actually lead God away must be a very beautiful one, for God to be taken-in by their tune means they are quite dangerous... But we must have broken our word. No wonder people were closing up their houses and fleeing, leaving them for the taking.

'It's an exodus,' Granny Irma says. 'They are not just leaving, they are fleeing. It's reached the stage that if they can't sell the very property they're so afraid of losing to the communists, they're just closing up and leaving it for the taking. I hear people are breaking into shut-up houses and settling in as if they were their very own, closed houses being taken over before the communists even arrive.'

'I would also leave if I had the chance,' Aunt Eileen said. 'Believe me, if I had the money I would also leave with Norma. This will be no place to bring up children. Can you imagine those people ruling the country? No, let me remain under the British... If I had the chance I would also leave. Stephanie, as usual you're blinding yourself to what's happening around you.'

'What would we do in those countries?' my mother said. 'End up as second-class citizens with very few rights, if any at all. No, let me remain here with all of its shortcomings. I will never leave this country.' She says that here she was born and here she will die, that this place is a little paradise but we don't even realise it, that living in England or America is no paradise but the people are foolish enough to think so, that's it's all a myth, that she loves this country even though unnamed, that this is her home, that we should stay and work things out.

'You don't know what you're talking about.' Aunt Eileen told her. 'What is there to work out? Tell me... '

Mother Carmelita also says the communists are going to take over. She said it in class today that they're the very devil itself.

'Do they come from hell?' I asked her.

'Don't be silly, child,' she said. 'Why do you have to take everything so literally.' 'Well, where are they coming from?' I asked, 'so that they can actually handcuff God and put him away like any common thief, the way Aunt Iris acted, even though there was no proof of it, but she did take the blows on her back without a cry as if they were her due, Granny Irma said... so that does make you think. I mean, why take the blows as if you deserve them without a cry?' Then I got all excited trying to make my point, so I also told her that neither has there ever been any proof of my great great grandparents' burial, only a verbal one of them fading fast, so is proof necessary, for everyone accepts that they are buried.

'What are you saying?' she asked. 'What's that about hand-cuffing God and your Aunt Iris and fading fast? What has gotten into you, Margaret?'

'I asked where are they coming from... where do they live? They must live somewhere.'

'Behind the iron curtain,' she replied.

'Behind an iron curtain? Oh no wonder they want to get out,' I said. 'I would also want to get out if I lived behind an iron curtain and go somewhere else, anywhere else, even to a place no one could put a name to. I mean, how do they breathe? Now I can understand why they want to come here and take over.'

I thought the other girls in the class would agree with me, but instead they laughed as if it was some big kind of joke, as if I'd said something very funny... One girl literally cracked up, she was laughing so much that even Mother Carmelita had to put a stop to it... Anyway I hushed up... it was no different to being slapped *whoosh* right across the mouth, so I hushed up.

But I thought she would understand what I was talking about, Arabella, but she only became quite angry and said I talked like a godless child and she must talk with my mother, for she's been noticing certain traits in me lately... Don't know what she meant and I preferred not to ask... She was already quite annoyed.

Mother Carmelita doesn't really care about me anyway, seeing my family isn't a wealthy Roman Catholic family and especially since I'm the sole Catholic in the family, only because I liked those beautiful peaceful statues from the beginning, statues that can come to life at any time and speak to you, like one did for Saint Theresa. I like holding the beads and rattling off the Hail Maries. I like the stories of apparitions to children, mainly children who are never believed, but who know it to be true, who know in the end that truth will tell. Aunt Eileen says that I'm not one of the Portuguese children and that makes a difference, that I'm too dark skinned... She says she doesn't understand why, thinks I must be a throwback because, looking at my mother and father and in fact the whole family, except for the throwbacks, I should be fairer. My mother heard her and became quite upset. Said Aunt Eileen is not to give me such false ideas, for false they are... that there is no race called the fair-skinned race, that in those same countries to which they are fleeing in a mass exodus they will learn... There you are either one or the other, there are no in-betweens... She says quite a few can't take it when they go and often return or have breakdowns... Even Aunt Eileen was speechless at my mother's reaction. She said it reminded her of the old Stephanie of long ago when she would fight for every inch of her ground... that is until that man came into her life and then got out of it...

But can you even begin to imagine such a thing, Arabella? Living behind an iron curtain? I wonder who lifts it up to let them out, it must be so heavy? It must be a very difficult job, must take thousands and thousands and thousands to do so... The people must be extremely tired of it and so decided to call together a conference like my grandmother wants to have right now and arrived at the conclusion that they must leave or they would die from the sheer weight of the thing... Yes, they must have laid a map on a table and looked and peered, when the leader suddenly shouted, 'Here, this place!' 'Where, where?' they all cried out. 'What is its name?' 'It has no name,' he shouted. 'But how can we go to a place without a name? Who will lead us to it? How will we ask for directions if we lose our way?' 'Ah,' he replied, 'that's the thing we may have some difficulties with, but once we find it, then it will be very difficult to find us for they will have no name to follow-up on... This nameless country is just what we are looking for. We will go there, we will go to this place. 'Why?' some of them asked. 'There are other places we can go to. 'Because,' he replied, 'besides going to a nameless country, we must also get as far away from the iron curtain as possible and this place, as far as I can see on the map, is not only very far away but it is also quite small, in fact just a dot compared to other places, so easily passed over, with only half-a-million people, so there is room for more. Just the place for us to find our breath again. Later we can decide what must be done.' 'Ah...' one of them said, 'it isn't as easy as you make it out to be. What about God?' 'Oh that is no problem,' the leader replied. 'You keep forgetting there is only one God, you talk as if there are many. We have already handcuffed Him here and locked Him away so how can He be anywhere else? Think for a change will you...?'

Not a bad story is it, Arabella... must try to include it in one of my compositions. Miss Butler thinks I'm quite good at telling stories. I think she takes to me, as Granny Irma would say. She actually told me one day I'm the best in the class, that I have the most vivid imagination when it comes to writing stories. She said she actually looked forward to my compositions... I have to admit I add a little here and there... Granny Irma says I'm prone to exaggerate... she isn't going to use the word lying, no instead she would call it exaggeration... I do add a little here and there I have to admit... wouldn't you?

CHAPTER EIGHTEEN

'I hope you children are seeing what's happening,' Granny Irma said. 'I know I don't have to say that to Margaret. But you, Adrienne, I hope you are noticing, taking it all into account. I hope you're seeing what happens when you don't take Jesus into your life. You may think you know everything but listen to me with a little more experience. Your Aunt Eileen is now having to sell beauty products from door to door in the hot sun like any common sales woman, swallowing the pride she flaunted for all those years and having to beg the same people she despised to buy something... anything... then having to beg them to pay up...'

CHAPTER NINETEEN

The night fell.

The old woman waited in the dark.

'What did you have to do, Kathleen, to bring him back from the dead?' His eyes pinned her to the past. Disembodied eyes that now pursued her in the cracks; there was no escaping them, like the child's eyes that reminded her so much of Iris's... Iris referred to as the dark one, whose eyes would leave a trail, making it easier to find her buried in the leaves of a book, focused on the word though rarely uttering a word, haunted by the eyes of the dead.

'The doctors had given up, Kathleen; it was just a matter of time and then like a miracle he began to revive. What did you do, Kathleen?'

'Why can't you let me go, let the living be? You've been dead all these years and yet you can't let go. You keep on persisting, insisting. I'm an old woman now. I no longer have the strength to deal with this. Why can't you stick with the dead like any normal dead person, die, and leave like your brother Ralph did. What is past is past... why raise up the ghosts? What difference can it make now, tell me?'

'What did you do to bring Compton back, the illegitimate son of your brother Stan... brought to you on a rainy day by an unknown woman. After that, I always felt afraid for you.'

'Why can't you let me be, John? You could have dealt with this while you were alive. Instead you wait when it's already too late... What difference will it make at this point? Things have already run their course...Your eyes lurk in the cracks giving me no peace, demanding what was only hinted at when you were alive, when the whole matter could have taken a different course. Am I to take all the blame? What about you? You were my husband, a man of strong will, in fact even referred to as tight-fisted... You were there through it all... Why didn't you say something from the start, if for nothing else at least for our daughters' sake? Yes, yes, you warned me but was that enough? How much did you make up to them for my lack of attention, lack of interest... perhaps... lack of love? How could I not love him after being told by Dr. Ward that I could have no more children, that is if I wanted to survive, so after that unknown woman came on that rainy day... in fact it had been raining for three days, causing the gutters to overflow and the yard to flood so that when she came she couldn't get in, and I remember calling out to Mr. Carlton to put some pieces of wood across the path so that the woman could walk across and come into the yard. For me, if not for you, it was a miracle that only one day after Dr. Ward's pronouncement, only one day after I went on my knees and prayed, I was then presented with this newborn baby boy by a woman I had never seen before, as small as this country is, and never saw again, and my womb leapt with joy and I praised the hand of God.

Yes, yes you never liked it from the start, this child brought to us from nowhere. Yes, you did question it but then your purchases caught up with you, your new acquisitions of property and land and business went to your head and began to take control. Your greed caught up with you as it did with me. Every penny mattered to you, every penny, never forgetting, reminding us of the terrible poverty you had grown up in, the hard life you had experienced, a life you would make sure never to return to if you could help it. You who lived by the motto... 'We ants don't borrow, we ants don't lend', hated by your workers for your hardness of heart... some said even cursed. I let it be, didn't care once it could help his future, my hopes, for in this family we have always had a weakness for boy children, for sons. So why do you keep behaving as if you carry no blame in this whole affair? At least you are dead but I am faced with it everyday by those two, their very lives witnesses of our neglect.'

'How did you do it, Kathleen? How were you able to bring Compton back from the dead, for that's what we all considered him... dead? I will not rest until you tell me. You sold the seven houses I left you, signed the business over to him and pawned almost the entire jar of jewellery which should have gone to Stephanie and Eileen. All that we worked so hard for, you sold for the sake of this boy who I could never accept, never love, for I could see certain signs from the start: the selfishness, the ingratitude. He took it all and what did you get for your pains but that six-lined note? Took it all as his due... his right... and what are our daughters left with since you made him the inheritor? Could do so because I trusted you, never imagined you would leave your daughters penniless, or I would have made other arrangements. Now it's falling apart, the one house that came from your family, brought here piece by piece and erected by my own hands, the house given to your mother by right, since there was never any record of her parents' death or burial, the only fact ever confirmed the fading... the house which Iris never left until the very day of her death, the house which only you can see falling apart no matter how you point... show... reason... How terrible it must be for you, Kathleen, that only you can see the cracks... and perhaps her...'

'Her... ? Who... ?'

'Margaret... Who else? She who never lets anything pass her, prying into everything, sneaking around, listening, looking...

perhaps her... But then who would listen to a child? So she can't be of much help to you can she?'

'... Sucked into love of him from the very start as you were sucked into your business interests and property and land, but I turned a blind eye to it all. Oh where does all of this lead us, tell me?'

'Who knows, Kathleen, but this I must know. How did you do it, how did you bring him back from the dead?'

I lay curled up under the bed. The spider crawled on the mattress spring. I am terrified of spiders, I can tell you, but dared not move. My grandmother got up from the bed and left the room. I crawled from under the bed. I followed her.

CHAPTER TWENTY

My mother's getting married, Arabella. She told the three of us today before going to work. It's the same man who has been coming to see her for the past three months. We were formally introduced to him later that same day. She was very brief. Just said to us, 'I would like you to meet Gregory Hoffmann... you can call him Gregory from now on,' and he, just as brief, only pulled his lips back.

He comes every evening at six pm to see my mother... always at six... so that Aunt Eileen calls him 'on the dot'. She says it's a good sign when a man is that punctual. She says the only time her husband wasn't late was for his death... Died before his time she says.

My mother meets him at the door. She pulls up two chairs to the window in the drawing room and there they sit like two silhouettes facing each other with the two casurina trees hovering in the background. They talk in very low voices. He walks up the street to our house with a cigarette perched at the corner of his mouth.

Because of the cigarette, Granny Irma says she will never agree to the marriage and will not attend the wedding... says from the day she saw him walking up the street to visit my mother with the cigarette perched in the corner of his mouth her spirit didn't take to him. Grandmother says her sister is ruled too much by her emotions. Cigarette or no cigarette, my mother borrowed money from Grandmother to go to America to buy her trousseaux. Grandmother seems pleased with the forthcoming marriage. She feels it will help my mother financially as he has a good job, and in case anything happens at least we will be taken care of without having to depend too much on her.

My mother seems fairly happy. I don't know what I feel except, if it makes her happy, well, that's enough.

I'm not sure if it's the baku who had a hand in this but it might be the case since for the past month I've been leaving him bananas and milk. I don't rule him out of anything. I've learned a few lessons and one is not to rule him out, not to take him and his pot of luck for granted. I am better prepared for the likes of him as I was for the shot that killed my father in a place called Brooklyn that I have only seen in the movies. I admit I did cry and I do think of him, but can you imagine how much worse it would have been if I hadn't known he was leaving for good, as that was no different to dropping dead, especially seeing he never dropped a line anyway... The shot only blew up the whole thing... that's all... Perhaps the baku isn't as angry as before, as full of hate as before because of the bananas and milk... and I know he's been taking it because it's always gone when I check... so perhaps he had a hand in this marriage and my mother's new hopes. But just in case, because I'm not taking any chances this time, I left him a note expressing my appreciation.

CHAPTER TWENTY-ONE

'Sydney Williams finally declared his hand,' they said.

'Sydney Williams declared he is a communist,' they said.

'I am a communist,' he declared at a meeting. He raised his hand in a fist and delivered the blow and it resounded throughout the country. His supporters raised their fists in unison so the blow was even harder to take.

A man is dragged off his bicycle on Hibiscus Street and beaten to a pulp because he wore a red tie and therefore was seen as a member of Sydney Williams' communist party. He was the father of six children and had worked for twenty-five years at the Ministry of Education as a messenger. Was said to be a quiet man. Well, he couldn't be as quiet as all that, they say. Still waters run deep, they say. A traitor, they say. Going quietly about his business when all along he was secretly a communist. What further evidence did they need than a red tie?

Sydney Williams' supporters retaliated. They dragged a twelve year old boy off of his bicycle and beat him to a pulp... he was left a shapeless mass of pulped flesh recognized by his parents only because of the clothes he had left the house with. They then went on the rampage and painted the town red. Three houses and a cinema were burnt down.

The haters of Sydney Williams and all he stood for retaliated. A bomb was planted on the ferry. It exploded in the middle of the river. Human parts floated on the water for days... the pieces could not be put together. What could be picked up was picked up, some by fish, some by men... Some families were left with a leg to grieve over, some a hand, but they were considered the lucky ones for some had to make do with nothing...

The preachers are shouting from the pulpits that the people must take a stand.

The politicians are shouting from the podiums that the people must take a stand.

'Red will only make them see red,' I said to Arabella. 'You will have to take cover for a while. If I fall and cut myself I will make sure to cover it up immediately.'

The soldiers are coming from England to save the country.

The soldiers are coming to save God and the Queen.

The girls are preparing themselves for the coming of the soldiers. Many of the soldiers are single men.

Granny Irma is preparing herself for the coming of Christ. It has all been predicted in the Bible, if only we would take the time out to read it.

The communists are taking over. God is going to be removed.

The pied pipers will take over. Attune yourself to the new sounds. We will be taken away from our parents.

The pied pipers will take over. They will replay the old tune and the children will be taken in once again.

Grandmother and Granny Irma will be put against a wall and shot as they will be thought useless. Upon their word of honour.

'You must not believe everything you hear. People in this country understand very little of what goes on in a communist country. They are influenced by England and America, though they understand so little of what goes on in those countries. We will not leave. Life is far more difficult in those countries. We have it very easy here. We would be like second class citizens in those countries. There is no need to run.' That's what my mother keeps saying.

CHAPTER TWENTY-TWO

Aunt Eileen just came home. She was covered in sweat. She kept wiping it off of her face and the black dye from her hair kept drooling, making splotches on her forehead so that when I saw her coming through the gate I thought it was Ash Wednesday. 'Don't be silly,' she said. 'How can it be Ash Wednesday?' She didn't go on about it though because I think she was just too tired.

'Look at my nails,' she said to Granny Irma, 'look at my hands, who would have thought that my hands could ever look like this?' Granny Irma didn't answer. 'Getting those people to pay up is not easy. They are always willing to buy but getting them to pay up is something else... Eyes bigger than their pockets.

'It's always a bad time for them. Could I come back next week, it will be better then... A bill came that they have either forgotten about or thought they had paid... always an excuse. Me, Eileen Gomez, having to beg these people for a favour, having to rely on them for my living... This country is going to the dogs... Anyone there to pick up the scraps will be there, for believe me only scraps will be left the way it is going... Having to put on a smile... who would have thought?' Granny Irma still didn't answer.

'The sun out there is baking hot. Saw Elma on my way back. She asked if I wanted a lift... Of course I turned it down, told her it was fine... You know her... mouth is as long as rope. If she ever got me into that car she would start prying. I know they suspect, perhaps they know, but they wouldn't hear it from me... Did any of them come around after Stephen died and things got bad... but she would be in the same shoes if anything ever happened to her husband, for she is just as untrained as I am... They will never get anything out of me. Oh no, they will never know of my situation. Margaret, you must learn from this... Always put a face on things, a cover. Dress... be smart... never let people know you don't have money, it only leads to eye-pass. She kept insisting, "Let me give you a lift, Eileen, you do look a bit tired and hot," in that high pitched tone she has... but not me... prefer to sweat it out in that baking sun than go into her car.' Aunt Eileen then turned to me, seeing she got no response from Granny Irma.

'So how's school, Margaret? Hope you're buckling down to your studies... Stop fidgeting like that, keep still! Norma says you don't seem to do much work at school, that sometimes you even look as if your hair hasn't been combed... ink on your blouse and socks. She says you often look quite untidy. You are a careless child... Take more pride in yourself, hold your back up while I'm talking to you. Don't slouch like that... A good posture is very important. Look at your sister and Norma, they both walk with their backs up. I think Mother Carmelita would like to see your mother when she comes back next week. I keep telling her she leaves you too much to yourself and I don't have the time to follow-up on you... We might be living in the same house but I don't have the time, but you're big enough now to take some pride in yourself... Besides your reading, I don't know what you do all day... I don't see you with any friends to talk of... You are getting out of control. I can detect the signs and in my opinion Stephanie should crack down before it's too late...

but Stephanie is in another world, does not pay enough attention to the little things, to details, but someone has to. Can't live in the clouds as pretty as they might be. One has to buckle down to the details. I'm really keeping my fingers crossed that this marriage wakes her up... I really hope he treats her well.'

CHAPTER TWENTY-THREE

My mother is coming back today from America. She's been away for one month and we missed her.

The house smells of polish. Rose polished the floors and Granny Irma put up new blinds. Adrienne cut roses from the garden and arranged them in vases for the drawing room. She is very good at the social graces, Aunt Eileen says. They are quite pleased with her and have all concluded she is going to be a beauty, that she is very graceful and ladylike and I could learn a few things from her. Granny Irma says Guy is bright and will go places, that Adrienne is a beauty, but what about me... what am I good for? She says I'm a late developer so perhaps it will come out eventually, but she doesn't think she will live to see it, that one day I will burst out and everyone will be taken by surprise, but she will most likely be dead by then.

I bought anthurium lilies for my mother to welcome her back. She likes flowers very much. I once bought her some artificial flowers and she hated them. Says they were not real. She puts aside money every Saturday to buy flowers from Mrs. Chin, then she comes back home and spends the afternoon arranging and rearranging them in her vases. I know she'll be pleased.

CHAPTER TWENTY-FOUR

We went for the drive to the airport to pick her up. We were all happy to see her. She was dressed in her favourite colour blue. I asked her immediately if she had brought back anything for me. She said no, she could only bring back herself and wasn't that the most important thing, as her luggage was stolen at the airport on her arrival and she had to buy things she hadn't planned on buying, that there she was standing next to her luggage and before she knew it, it was gone. 'I'm so unlucky,' she said. 'Your poor mother,' she said. 'I've never been a lucky person, nothing ever seems to work out for me.' Had to spend money that could have been used for other things but instead had to rebuy what she had lost. Money that wasn't even hers in the first place but borrowed for the occasion. Grandmother wasn't pleased; I could see it on her face.

'How could you not see who took your luggage, Stephanie? In America one has to be more watchful as you well know. I told you that before you left. I told you to be careful, and it's not as if you haven't gone there before... I warned you.'

'As soon as the thief or thieves saw my mother they knew she was easy pickings,' I said to Arabella. 'She's a giveaway... They just knew... it's the way she looks, the way she stands as if warding off an expected blow with her chin on her chest.'

'Has let herself become too retiring,' Aunt Eileen says, 'too shy, that's her problem. Can't judge who she's dealing with, takes it all at face value... Hope this marriage opens her eyes I really hope so.'

CHAPTER TWENTY-FIVE

'Yes, Mr.Carlton, what is it?'

'Dhis morning Ah notice dhat wood ants eatin' into dhe two beams under dhe kitchen. A really tink you should take a look, Miss Harriot'.

'Later, Mr. Carlton, later. As you'll notice I've not been feeling my usual self lately. Perhaps next week, but it's enough having to deal with the cracks. I really don't have the strength to deal with wood ants on top of it. Then as you know, my daughter is getting married again so I have enough on my mind. They all seem to think I have some money hidden away which I'm not telling anyone of. I just can't understand how that idea ever arose. I do have something put aside but that is just enough to cover any unforeseen event. I mean tomorrow something can happen to me and I would have to go into hospital. I'm an old woman now and at my age one has to be prepared for these things. I always tell my two daughters that they should always have spare nighties put aside just in case something happens... you never know... spare nighties... and a will... I just don't see why she can't have a simpler wedding... At her age who needs a big show? After all, it's not the first time she's getting into it... it's not as if she's still wearing rose-coloured glasses... those broke long ago... but they never listen... At least, Mr. Carlton, this looks like a sensible marriage. Mr. Hoffmann has a good job and a steady income... In fact, he intends to rent the upstairs flat so you must do a paint job on it. I meant to tell you before but with everything I forgot... I'm not the same, Mr. Carlton... It's a relief the flat will be rented; what with the raise in taxes and the general upkeep of the house I can barely keep my head above water... things have become so expensive, not like when I was a child... How the government expects a person to live I don't know. I'll check it later, Mr. Carlton, then we can talk about it...'

Money... money... that's all they ever ask for, but have I ever got any gratitude considering all I've done for this family? Ingratitude is all one is repaid with... Who can a person trust these days? When I bring up the house, does anyone listen or even offer to help?... At my age and still having to take care of everything... Now he's telling me about wood ants... Just a few months ago I had to change a beam because of wood ants... If it's not one thing it's another but who listens? When I bring up the cracks it's as if I'm going senile and don't know what I'm talking about. Their eyes show it, just like your eyes, John... but yours demand. Eileen's and Stephanie's turn away... Margaret's pursue and Irma's accuse... no escaping the eyes... Before I can even finish a proper sentence Eileen and Stephanie are already out of the room... Well at least, thank the Lord, Stephanie seems to be getting into a sensible marriage this time, at least Mr. Hoffmann has a stable job with a stable income... It's all right for Irma to say that's all I've ever thought of, but if it weren't for that thinking, as much as they despise it, where would all of them be now? On the street that's where... As you used to say, John, a man without land and property doesn't stand a chance. If I was as hard as my sister makes out I could have put them all out long ago, and received a regular rent which would remove most of my troubles... Didn't I add that flat downstairs for her and Eileen? At my age having to count every penny... Look at you... dead... died before all of this started... Everyday some new change... Now they're demanding independence from Britain... feel they can manage themselves. Look what I have lived to see... the statue of the Queen pulled down and broken into two pieces... All we worked for over the years, and I get the feeling more and more that it was energy wasted... no one to pass it on to... not that there is much to pass on now... and even what's left is not wanted.

At least she doesn't have to worry about the children's school fees and school books and uniforms, at least she'll be able to manage and she won't have to rely on me so much because I just don't have it... they all seem to think I do... Hope she makes a better go at this one... Charles did try in the end, I have to admit... Would have stayed with her and had a go at it if she had gone to America with him, but she wouldn't leave her children, insisted that the children go as much as he said that they could send for them later... Then she has this love for this place... refuses to acknowledge any other place... Now look where he had to go to be shot... always said he was too good-looking for his own good. From the start when she brought him here I didn't approve of him as you well know... As usual you had nothing to say, you were always a man of few words. Stephanie got that trait from you... From the beginning I used to tell you that women liked him, could see it by the way they looked at him... Even I, as old as I was then, knew as a woman, but then you were a man so perhaps you didn't see it... Then when I heard about the Sunday fêtes that his father held to raise money to pay for his rent it was too much... on the Sabbath holding boisterous fêtes, Gladys said, inviting whosoever, once they could pay... with that upbringing how could he be otherwise? But she loved him... George used to say after he came back from England that she couldn't help herself, that we must take the place into account... such an outpouring of love he could understand... Look at me, didn't I do the same for Compton, loved him excessively? Perhaps there was something after all in George's theory, although at the time I held no store by it...

Remember how surprised George was at the change he saw in her when he came back from England... Couldn't believe Stephanie was the same girl who once fought like a tiger cat... those were his very own words, remember. He said something had died... her eyes looked burnt-out, he said. She was standing at the top of the stairs pregnant with Adrienne at the time when he saw her, and according to him didn't recognise her... same features but there was a subtle change, he told us. I was standing behind him... couldn't understand why he kept repeating her name. 'Stephanie, Stephanie, is that you girl?' He said later to both of us that the fight was gone out of her but neither of us cared to look... By that time the marriage was already almost over and the women were already a big part of it. Charles was one person who couldn't help but yield to temptation... She seemed to go along with the various women but it was Mrs. Sharp that did it... For some reason, from the time she heard of that one, she took it badly. Do you remember how terrible it was? Oh that was a bad time wasn't it? She went to pieces, do you remember? Hasn't put herself together since then has she? The wagging tongues didn't help, did they? One woman actually sent her a picture of the two at a restaurant, then another called her on the phone if you remember... Place is too small, George used to say... also adds to the excess... One is too generous or too mean, no shades of grey, only outpourings... If we had seasons, perhaps limits would have been set, but without seasons we lost control... Man needs boundaries, he used to say... Do you know, she never reacted to that letter telling her about the shooting... She read it and laid it down and has not picked it up since... for some reason no one has... perhaps Margaret has... wouldn't put it past her... is into everything... The letter is still there... Called the children and told them their father had an accident and that was it... Well, thank the Lord she's making another attempt. Dear God, help my daughter, for we are in the palm of your hand... Perhaps we should have spent more time with them... We neglected our daughters. For what? I for Compton and you for property and land... Now look at both of them, both unhappy women... Dear God, bless this marriage, for she is trying... she's hoping that this time... Give her the chance, seeing our position... Give her the chance to start with a clean slate...

But this time there was no response... like talking to the dead, she said to him... his eyes remained non-committal... like when you were alive, she said to him... your only commitments were to property and land and money... You're not helping me with this one, are you? On standby as usual...

I crept away from Grandmother's door. I could hear Mr. Wood's dog barking and hitting against the small kennel. I leaned out of the window and blew a bubble of spit. Just as I thought, Mr. Wood's son had just returned home drunk as usual. He could hardly hold his bicycle up. He cursed loudly at his father, he cursed loudly at his dog... His dog responded his father didn't. The father barely spoke, according to Aunt Eileen, because of his son... A negro man who at the time, when it was almost impossible for a man of Mr. Wood's colour to make good, was able to build up a good taxi service but his son had drunk it out and now they were left with a house and two pens of chickens...

I'm going to the alley to catch some fish, Arabella. I'll soon be back. I'll go and get an empty jam jar... As it rained yesterday there'll be plenty of fish in the gutter... Rose says she'll give me bread crumbs to feed them... I'll go through Mr. Bone's paling, but I have to watch out for Granny Irma as I'm not supposed to go in the alley... She's in a bad mood... has been humming hymns all morning from the time she got up... heard her telling Rose that we'd better keep out of her way as blows will fly... Whistle if you see Granny Irma to warn me... You can at least whistle can't you, Arabella... you can at least do that?

CHAPTER TWENTY-SIX

My mother wore a beautiful beige dress for her wedding. There is a picture of the wedding in the evening paper. I cut it out and pasted it in my scrap book. There she stands before the cake with her new husband, GregoryHoffmann, Bank Manager. He is looking down at the knife as they are both about to slice into the cake. She is looking up at the photographer, she shows a broad smile. My mother looks beautiful... at least I think so and that's what they all said. I heard Aunt Eileen whisper to Aunt Pamela that it wasn't the same glow like the first time, but then one can't expect everything, that it was enough that she smiled.

Her friends are standing around the table. Aunt Pamela is looking at the photographer. Godfrey Jones, one of the guests, appears as if he is looking into space. Half of Guy's head is in the picture... the one eye you can see looks enlarged. He isn't pleased as he doesn't like how his eye looks... says it isn't his eye. Norma is just behind Aunt Eileen. Adrienne is standing next to Aunt Eileen who has her hand thrown over her shoulder. Adrienne's waist is pulled in very tight. She looks very pretty. Many people commented on what a beauty she is growing into, that she takes after our father when it comes to looks... not that my mother isn't also good looking, they hastily added. I am not in the picture as I was running around.

I didn't pick up much as there was too much laughing and talking and drinking and eating. The food was laid out on the new dining table... part of the new furniture my mother bought for the redecoration of the flat. All of the old pieces have been discarded. Many of the guests made comments on how elegant the flat looked. I kept going back for éclairs... Many comments were also made on how much weight I was putting on.

Grandmother sat down on the new sofa for almost the entire evening. She said her old legs couldn't take too much standing. She appeared quite relaxed and I think is pleased with the marriage. I think she actually put aside the cracks that day. Granny Irma did not attend, just as she had forewarned. She can't put the dangling cigarette out of her mind. Grandmother and Aunt Eileen feel her reaction is uncalled for and that my mother should get all the support we can muster.

Aunt Eileen later said, when it was all over, that Marie Bannister was into everything, minding everybody's business so she could go and talk about it later... Says she doesn't see why my mother ever invited her, knowing how dangerous that woman's tongue can be and knowing how she always envied my mother, seeing that no man, on looking at her, could ever desire to marry her, so that when Guy was born, even my mother, who was not usually like that, actually refused to let her see him as she was afraid Marie Bannister would put an evil eye on him through sheer envy and spite. She actually had the gall, Aunt Eileen said aloud, to bring up my father's name, may he rest in peace, but she, Marie Bannister, hoped he, Gregory Hoffmann, would treat her cousin well and not like a certain person whose name she would not bring up on such an occasion, may he rest in peace.

CHAPTER TWENTY-SEVEN

'She would keep bumping into them,' Grandmother said.

'Bumping into who? What are you talking about, Mummy?'

'Them... you know, Eileen, my mother's parents... Our mother told us that because they decided to absent themselves, to be as inconspicuous as possible so as to give her a chance to pick up a white man, any white man, they placed a curfew on their movements, stuck to the minimum... She told us she had to call out to them in order to find them or she would wait for the clock, as they stuck to a routine... ate at a specific time, went to the toilet at a specific time. Sometimes they would be right under her very nose and she wouldn't notice... before her very eyes and she wouldn't see them... Once even leaned against her father to rest her back and didn't know, thinking he was just a pole... So it was easy to bump into them as you can imagine. They were able to remain at a standstill for hours. The white men who would sometimes stay at the house would cast them aside as one would anything that got in your way, without even realising or were in too much in a rush to notice... Not that her parents would call out, she said... they would just remain exactly where they were cast... Apparently, they didn't choose appropriate spots to remain at a standstill... It could be any-where, she used to tell us, anywhere... that was the problem... so one didn't know where one would come upon them... That's why she tiptoed through the house... walked only on tiptoe, peering ahead, looking, looking... As children we were always being told to 'watch out, watch out, look where you're going'. You know, Eileen, we must be careful... They might be right here before our very eyes, under our very noses and we wouldn't even know. Look at Iris right here and we don't even pick it up... Don't you feel her watching... like John... I can feel them watching and waiting. They're using the cracks to do it, Eileen, using the cracks to get in get through... We must be watchful, Eileen... very watchful...'

'I'm telling you, Stephanie, she's changing... something is happening to her... it's so noticeable. You should have heard her today talking about her mother's parents and bumping into them, and that Aunt Iris and Daddy are right here, that they come through the cracks... and you should have seen her expression while she was saying it... Gave me the goosebumps. I mean if she were *that* sort of person it wouldn't be so bad, but Mummy is known for her practicality, not one for seeing spirits... Rather, she has always been one who deals in concrete matters. Her head is not one for the clouds... that was more Aunt Iris's portfolio... Now she's talking in a weird way... It's those damn cracks... How do we get it into her head that it's all in her imagination, that cracks are not appearing and her house is not tumbling down? I'm going to sit down and talk to her, Stephanie, even if you won't. It's only today I realised how far this thing has gone. I thought it would pass over but it's getting worse... No, this very day I'm going to have a talk with her... You're another one... you would just let it happen and not even look over your shoulder... '

'What do you expect me to do, Eileen... you know Mummy... she was always a stubborn woman, a hard woman to move. Do you think we can help in anyway? You can try... for me I don't think there's a thing we can do... It's her age... she won't be the first and she won't be the last... that's how she is...'

'Mummy, I just want to talk with you. I personally think you are worrying too much about things that are not worth taking on. I know you think cracks are spreading... Don't feel any way if I tell you this... but... there are no cracks... Try to get that into your head... Your house is fine... nothing is breaking up as you imagine. I think you are just tired and need a break... even Gladys Davis thinks the same and you know how close she is to you... Even if you don't listen to me you should listen to her. There are no cracks, Mummy... '

'Eileen, my mother used to bump into them and not even know her own parents. There they were right before her very eyes, right under her nose and she didn't know. They're using the cracks, Eileen. I'm not talking gibberish. Margaret knows... she knows even though she's only a child. She knows more than the grown-ups, more than you give her credit for...'

'Mummy, how can you rely on a child? If you said Gladys Davis or Stephanie I could understand, but a fourteen year old child... for a child she is as we well know... Margaret's head was always full of nonsense and that Rose never helped... To take Margaret seriously on this is crazy... Listen to me... How can you put Margaret over what I have to tell you?'

'The eyes, Eileen... they won't let go. I'm a marked woman, Eileen, I'm telling you, a marked woman... even the child, Eileen, even her... like Iris... just as if Iris has come back to haunt me... listen to me, Eileen... right before your very eyes...'

Arabella, do you know my great grandmother would bump into my great great grandparents, not even recognizing or seeing them, her own parents... The white men would bump into my great great grandparents and cast them aside like any old piece of furniture and not even notice the difference between flesh and blood and wood. The white men would eat with my speechless great grandmother and not even see her... Perhaps if she had spoken, said something, she would have started to fill the blank slate and they might have recognised the script... not all of them, but a special one would have seen the writing on the slate and taken heed of her... but she was speechless and uttered never a word, afraid that something uncalled for might leak out, so she pressed hard down on her tongue to prevent a leakage... I bumped into my mother the day she stood at the window watching my father leave for good, and she uttered never a word, speechless at his departure... Perhaps if she had said something it might have helped... perhaps... then the glass of water I held in my hand would not have spilled on the floor and her tears would not have spilled on the window sill and my father's brains would not have spilled in a bar at the crack of dawn in some place called Brooklyn that I've only seen in the movies...

CHAPTER TWENTY-EIGHT

He hit my mother right across her face. His fingers splashed themselves right across her face like a spatula. He hit her again as if once wasn't enough, just like in the movies when you drag out a drowning person from the water and try to resuscitate them... *slap... slap...*

Her head jerked sideways at the suddenness of the blows. At first she just took it, seemed to turn the other cheek, then she sprang at him. My mother sprang up like I had never seen her do before and was never to see her do again. Her eyes were burning bright like I'd never seen them burn before or was never to see them burn again. She clawed at his face, raking her fingernails downwards alongside his cheek... Oh my mother burned bright.

His face fell back at the suprise of it, his skin singed by the burst of flame. My mother burned bright for a few minutes and then began to sputter, but she rose up again and sprang again. He ducked his head and she caught the top of his head. Her fingers raked through his scalp. The blood leaked onto his forehead, down his cheek, onto his collar. She sputtered again, and in the sputtering, in the fight to burn bright, her body seemed to lose control. She frothed at the eyes, frothed at the mouth. She began to claw at the air, she dragged her nails along the wall... her body dragged downwards alongside the wall. She attempted to rise but fell back... She attempted again but fell lower... She attempted again but this time fell onto the floor... Her fingers raked the polish off the floor. She finally sputtered out. My mother, who burned bright like I had never seen her do before, sputtered out like I had never seen her do before. Washed up in her tearsuds and spitsuds.

'What happened to your face?' they asked him.

'A cat scratched it,' he replied.

CHAPTER TWENTY-NINE

Her eyes are almost at a standstill.
Her words are almost at a standstill.
Her body is almost at a standstill.

'It's everything,' Aunt Eileen said. 'I would also take it badly. Looking at her life, sometimes I can't help agreeing with her when she says how unlucky she is... the unexpectedness of his attack. With all of Charles' ways at least he would never hit her. Our hopes were too built up and we helped in the building... Irma said from the start that her spirit didn't take to him... A lot was at stake for this one, now she doesn't have much left to throw, does she? Who would believe it, the old dog... acting as if he couldn't mash ants and taking advantage of a helpless woman... He could have waited, but three months after he shows his true colours... Irma was right this time... this time she hit the nail on the head...'

'It's the cigarette,' Granny Irma maintains. 'My spirit never took to him from the time I saw him with that cigarette perched on the edge of his lips. I went straight to her that afternoon and told her, "Stephanie, don't marry that man, don't make the same mistake. You yourself know it's easier to get into a marriage than to get out of it. Don't take the money into account as my sister does. God will take care of you. I know that from experience... Once you get into this one, this time you will hardly likely be able to get out if it doesn't work... This time you will be stuck... You still have time... you are far from an old woman, you are still an attractive woman... There is no need to prove whether you're lucky or unlucky. Don't tempt God"... but then my sister didn't help... all she could see was the money. "The man gets a good salary, has a good job," she said. "She will be better off... The children are growing up; it costs more to bring them up... Who will pay the school fees, buy the school uniforms, take care of the daily expenses? She is just on the edge as it is... this marriage can pull her back from it." My sister says she can't continue to help in the same way... she has to protect herself... to think of Ruby, poor Ruby... ending up in a home the way she did. Who would ever have seen such an end for her... not Ruby herself. Well I said to her, man imposes but God disposes... but I don't know if she heard, just kept on how Gladys told her they actually had to break down the door and drag Ruby out of the house, drag her along the ground to get her to that old people's home... Apparently she screamed all the way. She keeps saying that I must think of it, but I tell her I trust in Jesus and I will be looked after, that she should have more faith, but she keeps on about her... Ruby... "Who?" one had to keep asking, "What's that?" her voice was so low... Screamed all the way until the day she died... Says she heard the nurses eventually had to strap her down on the bed and tape up her mouth and all because of money and no one to look after her... Did not even have the means to cover her burial... Without this marriage Stephanie will have to keep drawing on her as Eileen has started to do... She doesn't have it any more... down to one house and that one house breaking up before her very eyes and no one listens or even believes... How she can't carry her anymore... Ha, claiming that the house is breaking up and yet she doesn't learn... a house that never belonged to her in the first place, but was really the family house, but then she and her husband had the means to take it over... A house of spirits never laid to rest. I told her and John at the very beginning, when they made the decision to bring it into town board by board... I told them, smoke it out first, smoke out the spirits, let them rest first, but they were too preoccupied with property, too caught up with making money to listen, to even understand... Think of it, I told them... a house where two people are reputed to have faded away without a trace left... which our sister could not leave until death stepped in and took a hand, as if something held her there... would not leave that house... At least Stan used to visit her now and then, seeing he was the one who watched out for her, particularly with our father, then he ups and is killed by a man who apparently went beserk...'

'What a story that was... made the headlines... the man attacked fourteen people with a cutlass but only two were killed... Stan died on the spot. He was standing outside a rum shop which he used like a church... Can't ever remember getting a sober word out of him... Whenever anyone came to ask for him I used to say, "He's at his usual church..." "Oh," they would say, "has your brother turned to God? What a blessing, Mrs. Chase... You should thank God on your knees everyday". He was still my brother and I would defend him... the only one who dared stand up to our father, seeing not even the Governor himself was able to do so... It was rumoured that the Governor actually said it was a pity our father wasn't white...

'I used to tell them to smoke it out; it is not a good place... Let them be laid to rest... now all of us are caught up in it... I warned Stephanie from her first marriage. I told her, "Stephanie, do not remain here... go and start a new life with your husband... move out... if you don't, you will never do so". She tried... went for one year then when Charles was away, moved back without telling him so that when he returned things were back to the start... Superstitious, Eileen calls me... talking like Rose... it's that Church she claims... well I hope they can deal with the consequences... Now she tells me she is beginning to see Iris's eyes peeping through cracks, that John refuses to let go, would not die like any normal person after all these years... She prowls around the house at night looking for heaven knows what... yet she is still talking about the man's stable job and good income... When is my sister going to learn?'

CHAPTER THIRTY

Aunt Eileen says you came out straight from the bush. Everytime she says it, Arabella, I think of you as an arrow shot from the bow, spat out from the lips of the bow heading over the bushes, at first all aquiver, then suddenly swirling, heading up over the trees, up into the air, rushing and swishing and zigzagging over the forests and falls and mountains and rivers. Perhaps, perhaps, you got carried away and started to ascend higher and higher, all in a flourish piercing the clouds... Then that's where the trouble started... It really started going to your head, didn't it? You became charged-up just from the feel of it and in the spur of the moment decided to make a charge for the sun itself. The light bounced off of you and you caught a reflection of yourself and you looked no different to a rainbow... and you remembered how the trees called after you as you ascended, you remembered how the trees stretched and yearned to get where you were, but they were rooted and they bemoaned their roots, longed to break free of their roots so they could join you... they called to the wind to help them and it roared in reply and rushed up in a sudden blast and wound like ribbons around the trunks tugging and pulling but to no avail. Even the powerful wind couldn't help... and you laughed and your laughter echoed throughout the forests and the people heard it and thought they heard the sound of a bird calling out... That's when you really let it go to your head, didn't you... the fact that those mighty trees would envy you for the sheer mastery of the thing, that you could reflect the colours of the rainbow, that the powerful wind itself couldn't help...? So you plumed yourself in a mass of pride and vanity and charged for the sun, but it was too much for you, you went beyond yourself didn't you? So that's what stopped your tongue dead in its tracks and it hasn't recovered since... struck dumb... and to think I thought you were hushed up. In fact I would call it more dumbstruck... but even then you couldn't turn back because you were targeted for this house and whoever sent you off was a crack marksman. But this time you were on the descent, descending to my grandmother's house, this time all in a whirl and twirl. You plummeted and you're still recovering aren't you? It was too much for you, you just went beyond yourself, you went a little too far, but who knows, maybe I can help you out. I can use Granny Irma's bow that she has on the wall and if you ever feel the need to go back I can send you off like an arrow back to your village. You know the way and it should be easier the second time around... How would you like that, Arabella? Think about it... you never know... it might prove useful... Who knows?

CHAPTER THIRTY-ONE

The cracks were spreading. They were now in every room of the house, but with a difference. Before, she would just come upon one... her eyes would fall upon one... but now she actually knew the moment one was about to appear, for she would hear a swishing sound reminding her of the sound of the cane as her father brought it down to bear on the back of Iris, the sound of a scythe cutting grass... there was no placing it. She would block her ears to avoid hearing it, for it tore and scraped at the air leaving her heart in a flurry. She found it difficult to sleep at nights. How could she? Gladys said she needed a break, she should try to get away go to the country and have a rest, but get away. Gladys strongly felt Stephanie's marriage was not helping, seeing Stephanie decline before her very eyes and not able to do anything. 'I told her to leave him, Gladys, would you believe it? I told her to forget the money. I would help her with what I have... It wasn't easy to tell her because I don't have it, as you know, but I can't bear to watch her, the way he dogs her footsteps, shouts at her, actually hit her some weeks ago. In this family a man has never hit a woman, but he has set the precedent... We will manage somehow, I told her, even though God knows I don't have the wherewithal, but I don't think she even heard me. I don't think she cares any longer. She actually said she felt sorry for him, he couldn't help himself, he is what he is, we are what we are... It's also affected her children very much... they hate him. Margaret is wilder than ever.

'Rose, you must cobweb the house... the cobwebs are all over the ceiling... the crocheted web is in the trunk.' How could she have forgotten it... the crocheted web made by her mother that still lay in the trunk in her bedroom? How could she have forgotten it? Why hadn't she thought of it before? That was the very thing to use to catch the culprit, to get to the source. She could throw it out and, one never knew, she might catch something... Why hadn't she thought of it before?

Grandmother asked me to help her go through the old trunk in her bedroom to find the crocheted web made by my great grandmother a long time ago when she was shut up in a waiting room, awaiting the footsteps of a white man, and to fill the time she crocheted a web along the same design as the spider's web which hung over her bed on the ceiling, and which no one could bother to sweep away, and it was that web that helped my great grandmother to catch her husband and with which my grandmother hopes to catch the culprit. I am very afraid, very afraid...

I took money out of Grandmother's purse while she was asleep. I went quietly into the room, walking on the boards that don't creak. I'm so good at it I can tell instinctively which boards would cry out. I opened her purse very quietly and took out enough money to buy him as many bananas and milk as he wants... The baku must be fed... If I have to borrow or steal I will have to feed him... My mother is now almost at a standstill. I must get her to burn bright again... My only hope rests with him. I haven't seen him for a while, but I must get those bananas and milk. I am very afraid for her. I am very afraid that Grandmother will catch him with the crocheted web before I can help my mother. I can't allow it to happen. I am very afraid for her... She lay down on my bed last night and cried... I could hardly bear it... she slept on my bed last night she was that unhappy... I must take measures to help her... anything once I can help her.

CHAPTER THIRTY-TWO

'You see it's getting worse don't you?' she said to him. 'What did we do? What have I done? Gave my life for Compton and got only a six line note... sold all we worked for so he could make something of himself and in the process cast my daughters aside. They are trained for nothing, helpless without husbands, unable to fend for themselves. I loved him and in my love neglected them but you could have helped.'

'How did you do it to bring him back from the dead, Kathleen? Did you do it at the cost of your daughters? What did you do to bring him back from the dead those three weeks you neglected your house, your daughters, me? You fought like a tiger for his life. He owes his life to you and what did you get for it except a six line note and this.'

'She is even more unhappy now. This marriage is a disaster. But the town is small, so how can she admit to them that this one also failed, if they don't already know. They wait on the sidelines like vultures ready to feed on anyone's unhappiness, for they have so little to occupy themselves. She always had an excessive pride and at least that still burns. It would take a person of great strength to admit another failure. Abandoned by her husband for another woman, a man she loved too much from the start, a man too goodlooking for his own good, a man that women couldn't help falling for... She loves him still, dead as he is, for it is branded into her very soul. But she made an effort after all by marrying this man, for she must have hoped this could ease it... She hoped, but this one is no good... You have remained very quiet lately except for the usual question... How come? Are you beginning to think of the part you played, dead as you are? Her sadness weighs on my heart for the first time when it is perhaps already too late... Then there is Eileen... I guess she will survive... Perhaps selling beauty products door-to-door, pleading, persuading people to buy creams and perfumes and shampoos and conditioners will open her eyes to the changes... She lives hand-to-mouth but is still as pretentious as ever... perhaps that trait will help her in the end... who knows?'

My grandmother started to cry. Soundlessly the tears drooled along her grooved face. My eye pressed against the crack. The water dripped onto the potty... plop plop plop... so that was what grieving was about after all, just a plopping sound. Now I could see why the last time I heard it I couldn't place it... Plop plop plop...

CHAPTER THIRTY-THREE

He doesn't even touch the bananas or milk, he leaves everything right there. His skin looks like hardened cracked-up mud, he refuses to eat, he's that spiteful. His calabash head seems to have grown larger, as large as his head can grow considering his size. His hair is all gone... He keeps harping back to the past. Says it's too late to do anything and I will regret it. I plead and cajole but he doesn't even listen, Arabella. 'Help my mother, it has nothing to do with me. She isn't to blame, it's me, forget me, think of her. I will get as much bananas and milk as you want but just help her. I will never leave you hungry again. I actually stole money from my grandmother, something I have never done before and hope never to do again, just to keep you happy. I am no different to a thief, no different to Aunt Iris. I will now have to go into hiding just like Aunt Iris and all because of you. I didn't understand, after all it was the first time I had to take care of a baku. How did you expect me to know?' I said to him. 'I am just a child. I only heard about you through Rose and Mr. Carlton. How did you expect me to know?' But his eyes are hardened mudballs. He frightens me. He actually spat at me, spat at me, then began to pelt me with stone-words again. 'Get away from me, get away from me!' I must think, Arabella, there must be a way out. How do I get rid of him before he kills my mother, before my grandmother catches him...

CHAPTER THIRTY-FOUR

Rose ran up the steps.

'Where yuh grandmudder?'

'In her room,' I answered.

'Lawd, Ah don' know how a goin' to tell her dhis one. She have enough on her plate a'ready widout addin' dhis'.

'What happen, Rose?'

'Is Mr. Carlton.'

'Mr. Carlton?'

'A jus' come from his house. He not comin' back. He decide to join dhe new political party. He say times changin' and he can' work as a carpenter no more. Ah couldn't believe was dhe old Carlton... If yuh see him talkin' to dhe people wid a lot a verve, usin' words Ah never hear him use before. He say times changin' and is his people time now. Ah tell him to tell Miss Harriot herself but he is a coward. Joinin' party to change dhe country and yet he can' even tell her dhat he not comin' back. Dhis one goin' to really hit her. Mr. Carlton work wid she and her husban' from early, before dhey even own any house or lan'. Lawd dhis one goin' to really hit her.'

'Well, well. She never even answer when Ah tell her. Is jus' like she don' hear. All she speakin' 'bout is dhe noise like somebody cuttin' grass or cane. If Ah can' hear dhe breakin' up of dhe wood. Ah say to her as gentle as Ah could, 'Miss Harriot, Mr. Carlton say to tell you he not comin' back to work as yuh carpenter. He say he join dhe new party an' he won' have dhe time to work wid you anymore.' But she didn't even bat an eyelid. All she do is cock her head one side like she hearin' someting.'

'Ah say to her, "Miss Harriot, yuh hear what Ah say?" But all she reply is, "Rose yuh hearin' it? If yuh lis'en very carefully yuh might hear it." Well how Ah could tell her a don' hear a ting... so Ah say, "Yes, Miss Harriot, Ah can hear it also." "What it sound like to you?" she ask... To her is a sound she can' describe to anybody... She say dhe only ting she can tink of when she hear it is like someting cuttin'. So Ah tell her it sound dhe same to me, jus' like she say. Ah couldn't get anyting else from her. Dhen she say she goin' to catch dhat culprit tonight if is dhe las' ting she do. She say wid dhat piece a crochet she take out from her mudder ole trunk it goin' to help her catch dhat culprit... She must catch dhat culprit or dhe situation goin' to drive her mad.'

CHAPTER THIRTY-FIVE

'It's coming to the end,' Granny Irma said. 'It must be coming to the end. If you read the Bible you will see it's all been predicted... wars and rumours of wars, earthquakes, brother against brother, sister against sister, wife against husband, husband against wife... We will see it and we must be watchful... Look at my sister. Gave her life to land and property and look at what's happening to her now. All what she gambled on falling to pieces and she can't do anything about it. The son she was so obsessed with gone, not even bothering to look back... her husband was hard as nails... they were so similar in outlook now he's dead and gone... Her daughters' lives in a mess... Your mother, Margaret, is in trouble. I won't be surprised if something happens to her... Don't like how she's looking. You poor children like orphans with no father and a stepfather that my spirit never took to... My sister and I are old so it's not as if you can depend on us. I, for one, already have nine toes in the grave and one on a banana skin. My sister seems to be losing her mind... can't handle what's happening. This house is not a good one, I said it from the start... Smoke it out I said... but they didn't have the time to listen... everything seemed so secure with them... how could they foresee this... They seemed so on top of everything... Married to a man of strong will with the Midas touch... everything he laid hands on became his, changed into money... The son she always wanted doing so well at school with a brilliant future before him, the son that was to continue what they had begun... Now it's evaporating before her very eyes and she wasn't prepared... Thou fool, tonight thy soul shall be required of thee... Went to church every Sunday, never missed a service, but did she ever ponder on those words? At least I cut my losses when my husband left me a pair of scissors... at least I was still young enough to do so, but my sister is old and it's more difficult to do it the older you get... the energy goes... She seems to be aging overnight. Now Rose is telling me Mr. Carlton is not coming back... loyal Mr. Carlton has deserted... look what I have lived to see.'

'Margaret, pass the knife for me. I keep telling you children cake is to be eaten as dessert not as food... It's not meant to fill you. This is the last slice you're getting. Instead of eating proper food you're filling your stomach with all sorts of unnutritious things. I don't like how your mother is looking. I for one will have nothing to say to that man. I don't want him in this flat and if he ever hits her again I will fight him with my bare two hands as old as I am, but I will fight him as long as I have breath in this body. I will take my shoe heel and hit him right on his head... believe me I would do it. You children are now seeing me as an old woman... if you had seen me in my youth... I was a striking woman. If I'd had the opportunities I see women having now... if I'd had... Do you children know I once went to live in America? Spent six years there... but my pride couldn't stand it... my heart would twist everytime I was made to sit at the back of a bus. The first time it happened I couldn't believe it... the bus driver said, 'Go to the back of the bus, nigger'. I sat in front not knowing... How could I, coming from this country where the bus driver actually waits for me to sit down before driving off, where he would even hold the bus for me... They all know me as Mrs. Chase... Then to be told to sit at the back of a bus because of my colour, my race... not me... no, I couldn't live in that country. I packed up and left. Mr. Hoffmann... daring to hit my niece... and where he got that name from I don't know... Who ever heard of such a name? Hoffmann. I saw him the other day and I walked past him as if I had never seen him... daring to hit my niece... with all the problems we've had, no man has ever hit a woman in this family... It's the end... the Bible says it...Look what's taking place in this country... People are leaving in droves... Hear the Woodhouses' are leaving for Canada... imagine them leaving... All the skilled people are going... running as fast as they can... fighting and burning... Pray, we can only pray... that I would live to see my sister in this state... who could ever have predicted this?'

'Why, Sister Thompson, how nice to see you... Margaret, bring a chair for the Sister... Well, I haven't seen you for a little while... Heard your mother isn't well... so how is she doing?'

CHAPTER THIRTY-SIX

My mother asked me to feel the lump in her breast. She said she was putting on deodorant when she felt a lump. I woke up and saw her in the mirror with her hand raised above her head. She looked at me and said, 'Margaret, come and see if you feel a lump right here.'

'Your mother has to go into the hospital to have some tests done.'

'Irma, Irma, that was Stephanie on the phone. She was crying. "Mummy, Mummy, the cyst is malignant." Irma, did you hear me?' Grandmother said, sitting on the steps.

'What's going to happen? What will happen to these children with no father,' Granny Irma said, joining Grandmother on the steps.

I began tapping my fingers to the sound of my beating heart.

They've removed her breast and she returned home with a lopsided chest. My stepfather continues to shout at her. He hasn't changed much. I hate him but not as much as I hate that baku...

I began tapping my feet to the sound of my racing heart.

She is in pain most of the times. You can see it in the way she keeps pulling her arm up and down. The doctor says that's inevitable... that she must remember that she has had a major operation, but fortunately the cancer was caught in time... that it is important she keeps exercising the arm... Early detection of breast cancer is extremely important... it's a matter of life and death.

I began dancing to the sound of my throbbing heart.

She bought a sponge breast and puts it in her bra to fill it out. It's hard to tell the difference...

CHAPTER THIRTY-SEVEN

A vase broke last night. Grandmother cast the crocheted web out before her and caught it on the table and dragged it towards her. Said it looked like a dwarf sitting on the table, like a little person sitting there, but it was too dark to tell and she thought she had the culprit, was sure she had gotten to the source of the cracks so she threw all caution to the winds and threw the crocheted web out before her... said it billowed out and in fact looked quite beautiful, like a fisherman's net... Said she pulled it towards her and then there was the crash and splinters and breaking.

But she says she could have sworn it was a little person, that high, sitting on the table.

CHAPTER THIRTY-EIGHT

I'm in a lot of trouble. I stole money from a girl at school to buy bananas and milk because of the baku, because of her, because of whatever you may think, Arabella. Mother Carmelita called my mother and said she would like to have a meeting with her. I have been suspended for three weeks. I find it hard to believe I did it, but I did, just like that.

Elizabeth Marks left her desk for a moment... She comes from a very well-off family and is the only child. She is made quite a fuss of in school... not surprising. Aunt Eileen says the Portugese children are treated royally, especially when they have enough money to make donations to the Catholic Church. She says the likes of me hardly stand a chance unless I have the brains or colour to fight it, and seeing I'm not the brightest or fairest, my chances are almost zero... Elizabeth Marks always has money, so I decided to do it on the spur of the moment... It's not as if I planned it... As she left the desk to go the library I pretended to be picking up something from the floor. In the meantime I went into her school bag and, as luck would have it, or what I thought was luck at the time, my hands fell on her purse immediately... Well, as bad luck would have it, she came back a little while later and for some reason went into her bag to get the money... Oh did she raise a fuss. 'Someone has stolen my money,' she said in front of the whole class. She said 'stolen', in such a superior way, as if she were glad, for here was an ample chance to prove her superiority. Miss Pratt heard her... How could she not, it was said so distinctly... Miss Pratt also seemed glad, the way she reacted. She clothes-pinned her nostrils in the way only she can... I have tried it out a few times but don't have the nose for it... She pronounced each syllable the way she emphasises we should, just as if she came straight from England, Aunt Eileen says, and you can bet she never went further than the jetty. 'We will search everyone's bags and pockets immediately,' Miss Pratt said. Well, you know the rest... So here I am... I must admit I almost fainted... I felt my disgrace, believe me...

Miss Pratt going on and on about how could you do such a thing, Margaret Saunders... how could you do such a thing... This school does not cultivate thieves, we cultivate girls of high moral character, girls who hopefully will have a vocation... I just stood there, I was speechless... me... not able to say anything. Can you believe that, Arabella? When Aunt Eileen asked me what I had to say and I told her nothing she actually softened a little, said it must have been bad for me not to say anything, I who can never stop talking... always having to be told to hush up. Mother Carmelita had me sent to her office. She reared her head and hissed... How could I? It is not possible that a Catholic girl could stoop to this...It is a disgrace... I, who have had the privilege to have been accepted into the Roman Catholic Church... who every day is given instructions in the only true faith... I, who through my baptism into the Church have been marked for life, a mark that is invisible to the human eye but from which I will never be able to escape... a privileged child who is taught the scriptures everyday and made to say the rosary... that with all of this I should stoop so low as to take money out of someone else's purse... that girls in this school do not do this and for this I deserve to be expelled if it were not for my mother, who she has been told, is not at all well and could hardly take her daughter being expelled for thievery...

'I must tell you, Margaret, there have been complaints from various teachers. They have been telling me that you have not been your usual self, that you hardly pay attention to your schoolwork, that you are not giving in your homework, that it is difficult to get through to you... Apparently you have been found many times reading a book in class when you should be doing other work, that you have been acting strangely. As soon as your mother is better, I will have to speak with her, Margaret. In the meanwhile, you will be suspended for three weeks... Think it a blessing that we have decided to keep you here... We have the reputation of this school to think of and uphold... What will Elizabeth's parents think? Will they say we are nurturing this type of person in this school? You are fortunate we will not expel you and we are not doing so only because of the precarious health of your mother, which I cannot fail to stress... '

Granny Irma says I'll send her to an early grave, that it's a disgrace that a member of her family should be caught stealing like any common thief, that if I had wanted money why hadn't I asked? I am not starving, she said. She says its those books I've been reading, giving me all sorts of ideas, that I am growing up like a little heathen and that the Catholic Church doesn't help. She says praying to those statues is no different to praying to graven images and the Bible warns us against this. But who listens to her, she says... she is no different to a voice crying in the wilderness... Oh, it caused quite a furore. Granny Irma exclaimed, with her mouth curved downwards, that Stephanie's daughter will send her to her grave before her time...

Aunt Eileen says she doesn't know which way to look it's so embarrassing... says Norma couldn't go to school for two days she felt so ashamed. Caught red-handed, Aunt Eileen says, going into Elizabeth Mark's school bag and taking out her money... Oh the shame of it. That their friends have enough to talk about in this family without adding this, and suppose Marie

Bannister heard... just suppose... This she refused, absolutely refused, to even contemplate... Imagine the people she sold her beauty products to hearing about it... Suppose any of their children went to the convent... Her niece a thief... She says she keeps telling my mother I'm left too much on my own, that I need more supervison... but to actually go into someone's purse and take out their money... How could I even think of such a thing? What got into me to think of such a thing? How selfish I am... That in fact I should be trying to do as much as I could for my mother at this time... that our mother has enough to bear without making it even worse... Can't I see what she's going through, that this would only add to her shame... shame of two failed marriages and then her own daughter a thief...

My mother didn't say anything... didn't even bring it up. She came in late the same evening they found out and heard me crying because I heard her asking Granny Irma. I thought she would come in the room and speak to me but she didn't, she didn't say anything. I heard her go to her room... I feel so bad... I must have done a terrible thing...

CHAPTER THIRTY-NINE

I tell you, Arabella, something has taken over my mother's body. Just imagine, in only one month. I should not have left... How could I be so taken in by the baku... thinking I could go with Rose to see her old father. How was I to know he would act so quickly... Oh, I certainly underestimated him. Arriving back with no idea and then being greeted with the news that she had gone to see the doctor, so you can imagine how I felt when I saw her coming up the path, shuffling step by step by step by step. I tell you, Arabella, something has taken over my mother's body, something has crawled into my mother's body, something has crawled into my mother's eyes. She was cradling her swollen charcoal log of an arm against her lopsided chest, hugging the piece of charcoal, not letting go of it, holding onto it for dear life as if it were a dead child. She was being led up the stairs by Aunt Eileen and Granny Irma. I literally came to a standstill... In one month something has taken over my mother, crawled into my mother. Her eyes drown her face... bruised eyes... oozing eyes... long distance eyes... bulbous eyes just at the bubbling... We are now no different to two strangers. I tell you, Arabella, with all my prying and snooping and listening, I wasn't prepared for this one. Aunt Eileen and Granny Irma led her to her bed. Grandmother sat and watched as if she didn't have the strength to get up.

'Rose, Rose, go and bring the bedpan,' Granny Irma called.

'I will not use a bedpan,' she said, 'I will not use a bedpan.' So instead she threads her way to the toilet... her blue nylon nightie hangs on a threadbare body... her hair a halo of scattered threads... eighty-five steps to get there and one hundred steps to get back, since she had to make an extra U-turn around the bed.

'It's all right, Stephanie, just lie here. Everything is all right.'

I can no longer look at her. But try to understand, Arabella, I mean something else was in that room that has no connection to her. The baku has ambushed her and taken her away. He left something else in its stead so I avert my eyes.

'Are you in pain?' Adrienne asked her. She does not reply. 'I do not wish to see him,' she says. 'I cannot let him see me like this. Do not let your friends come to see me. I cannot let them see me like this. Do not tell your friends I am ill. I cannot let them see me like this... Are you afraid, Margaret? Are you afraid of your own mother?'

'No, I am not afraid of my mother... But you are something else which crawled into my mother and has taken over, removing her. No I am not afraid of my mother but I am afraid of you, for you are not my mother that I left one month ago. My mother was all right one month ago, though precarious, still all right.'

'Buy me a can of pears, Margaret. I like pears very much, as you know.'

'Eat the pears!'

'No, I don't want any. Hold me up, Adrienne, Margaret, Guy, hold me up... your poor bruck-a-duck mother.'

'Do you wish orange juice... Why don't you drink some orange juice, it's good for you?'

'Oh my God have mercy on me... help me... the pain... the pain... Oh my God... I can't stand it... help me, Oh God.'

'Are you in pain?'

'No... I'm not in pain. My children, what will happen to my children?'

'I will never leave you, children... I will never leave you...'

'I saw a jumbee bird yesterday afternoon; it was on the window sill. I heard Mr. Wood's son's dog howling all of last night. I could hardly sleep... Your mother is getting worse, she will not live... Your mother is dying... your mother is sinking fast.'

My brother can hardly sleep because of the sound of her rattling chest... My brother is all rattled... My mother is not dying, my mother will be fine... 'Hail Mary full of grace the Lord is with thee blessed are thou amongst women and blessed is the fruit of thy womb Jesus Holy Mary Mother of God pray for us sinners now and at the hour of our death amen.'

Fear-swollen eyes, eavesdropping eyes, splintered eyes making all that fear mixed with never-before-encountered things bubble over, leak out... drip... drip... drip... drip... all over the house... drip... drip... drip... causing a leakage... drip... drip... drip... drip... drip... drip...

'Oh God, Margaret, I can't breathe, I can't breathe.'

'Granny Irma... Grandmother... Aunt Eileen... Adrienne... Guy... Rose... Arabella... my mother can't breathe, she can't breathe... Help my mother... help... help... her...'

Baku... baku... where are you? Why didn't you tell me what you are capable of... I didn't understand the day I heard Rose and Mr. Carlton talking about you... How was I to know... I was only a child. Baku... baku... I would do anything anything for you, anything to save her, but he says it's too late, that all he wanted were bananas and milk, not much, that's all... For all the luck in the world he only demanded bananas and milk, that little do I know what a person would give for all the luck in the world, that a person would sell his very soul for it, but did he demand my soul or anyone's soul? No... he would never do that... no... he never asked for anyone's soul though he could have done it... and could still do it... No... all he demanded were bananas and milk, as simple as that, but even that I couldn't give him. Instead I left him without food for one month. He whittled down to skin and bone, but what did I care? No... it was too late. I should have known what I was getting into before I got into it, that I should not have rushed into it the way I did, bringing him here, based on one conversation, not finding out anything more, that I have received my just deserts and I have no one else to blame but myself... Baku... baku, what can you do? He is leaving, he said... leaving for good... He will not say when but he will leave when it is all over.

I now walk around with an umbrella because of the leakage. I have to step very carefully to avoid the puddles, very carefully. You can't blame me, can you? I will put an umbrella over you, Arabella, so those things I can't put a name to... except for the fear... but all those strange things... wouldn't leak out onto your beautiful colours, for I'm not sure what they might do to your beautiful colours. I asked my grandmother if she wanted to share my umbrella and she said yes, and I didn't even have to explain why.

'What is the child doing? Close that umbrella at once. Don't you know it's bad luck to open an umbrella in the house... Why in heaven's name are you walking on your toes... Oh, I am too tired to have to deal with this now... Later... I just don't have the time now.'

CHAPTER FORTY

'Well, it appears this is it, doesn't it?' she said to him. 'Our daughter Stephanie is dying. This is it, isn't it? That I would live to see my own daughter die, that I had taken it for granted that my daughter would one day bury me. Is this the price I pay for my love of a boychild brought to me on a such a rainy day that the yard was flooded and I had to call out to Mr. Carlton to place strips of wood across the path, so that the unknown woman with a bundle could cross over. "Miss Harriot, Miss Harriot, Ah have sumting fuh you." Or was it our preoccupation with property and land and money and business... not that it was bad in itself, but then it became the only preoccupation, and greed became the norm. That he was only a part of my ambition, for he was a brilliant boy with a brilliant future who would increase what we had gained and worked for. Or was it that fateful night...?'

'What fateful night?' he asked.

The sounds drum on her eardrums, drumming out all other sounds except for his voice, persisting, insisting... What fateful night...? His words drum out all other words.

The swishing sound the cane made as it fell on Iris's back. 'You slut!' their father shouted, 'Nothing but a common slut... no wonder always acting like any common criminal.' Stan grabbing the cane out of their father's hand, shouting, 'Leave her alone, you goddamn bully, leave her alone' ... Their mother crouched in the corner... Iris allowing the blows to fall without a cry of protest as if they were her due... 'Get out of this house, Stanley, do you hear... Get out... out... and never step foot in it again as long as your mother and I are still alive.'

'My thoughts strayed, John,' she said to him. 'I'm speaking of the night the doctors finally gave up for his life? You should remember... you were there... you saw me... I would have killed for him at that moment... '

'Stephanie is dead. Stephanie is dead. It is 2:30 a.m. in the morning and Stephanie just died... Very quickly she sank like a stone without a murmur, leaving just a ripple in the wake of it. Stephanie is dead... Margaret, Margaret... what are you doing... what is the child doing? She's hitting the body, she's hitting and hitting the body... the face. She's dead, Margaret... What are you doing, what are you saying? The poor child... take her away.'

Burn bright... burn bright again... like I never saw you burn before... *slap slap slap slap*... Burn bright like you burned that night when he hit you, splashed his fingers across your face.

'Stop her, stop her, she's out of control... Stop the child... she's hitting her mother... Pull her away... take her away from the room... the child is breaking-up. What is she saying? She has been spending too much time alone. I kept telling all of you that. Take her away; she can't stand it.'

My mother finally sputtered out. No amount of hitting could set her afire again. She looked herself again, for she was once again at a standstill... that thing had crawled out of her but it had taken her breath away with it... She is now at a complete standstill... but at least I can recognise the traits.

CHAPTER FORTY-ONE

The sound is unbearable, it throbs on her eardrums... goes on all night without cease. She casts the web out in spurts but it is useless. Perhaps it's telling her something, perhaps it will tell her the source of it all, what it is all about... perhaps it's the sound that must be caught, perhaps there is no culprit after all... Oh, she is old... she is an old woman, tired and useless... How can she deal with this at her age...? She can no longer manage. 'Is it the sound I am to listen to,' she asked him... 'Help me... you are there... I am here... Why should I have to deal with this alone...? The blame also rests with you... it could not only be me. I am no longer young, my brain is no longer active. I am already out of things... Why me? Our daughter is now dead... How did it get to this? Where did it all start...? Was it Compton...? Was it the night I hid the telegram telling me of Iris, that she was dying the very night he lay dying, a babe in arms? Was not his life worth more than hers, had she not lived hers already, a woman not even considered in her right senses, a woman who never stepped out of her parents' house after their deaths until death stepped in, a woman whose life already appeared useless, a woman already laid on the shelf if it weren't for Stan? He always loved her and perhaps she loved him, who knows? Okay, okay, I can't take it anymore... Oh God, your eyes are killing me. Perhaps if I tell you, you will leave me alone... You have made me into a marked woman with your endless pursuit... Okay, what did you do Kathleen, what did you do? Well, here you have it just as you suspected but would never voice... Yes... yes... Compton... Compton... he was their child... Now, are you satisfied? Compton was Stan's and Iris's child. Now will you leave me alone, let me rest? I can't take it anymore... A child of sin... And what could she pass on to him but shame and book knowledge and where would either get him or her or any of us? Wasn't it better for her to die than live with the shame which would be passed on to us?... Think of it. After all, she was the one who sent him to me, so perhaps she wanted it like that... At least, this is what I consoled myself with through all the years. She wanted it, I said, for why would she have him sent by a woman never to be seen again as small as this country is... Stan killed by a man gone beserk, so who would ever give her the support she would so desperately need in this place... I couldn't... Perhaps I might even have lost you, for you were a hard man. So I hid the telegram... and the bird didn't help... that huge vulture bird that kept hitting and knocking at the child's cradle... I was half awake and half asleep when it came... The bird flew into the room, its claws heading for the baby... encircling the cradle of this baby delivered to me out of the blue after Dr. Ward told me that I could have no more children if I wanted to survive, which meant I could never bear a son, and in this family we have always had a weakness for sons... So would I not fight for his life? So I shouted to the bird, 'Go to her... take her... take Iris in exchange for his life... take Iris... a shamed woman, a damned woman in the eyes of God and man... One life in exchange for the other... Leave me him but take her... So I hid the telegram for two days and by the time we got to the house it was just in time to watch her die. I hoped she would already be dead for I feared her eyes... always did... but she didn't even recognize me, just kept repeating that they were there under our very noses, the ones who had faded fast with no written record of burial... the ones who had allowed the moths to take over, leaving fear-holes behind... the ones who had never been laid to rest... How could she leave them, she said, for they still suffered so much, for they were the ones who first told her that their grandmother was raped by some white man passing through the country that no none ever cared or bothered to put a name to... and, in the passing, kicked down a door, kicked down a man and kicked down a woman... The door remained but only the shells of the man and woman got up... shell-shocked... leaving behind a child later named Hope Amelia Hinckson who could pass for white... She said she remained with them from the time they showed themselves to her, they who had become invisible even while alive, who daughter and servant and white man cast aside like any old piece of furniture, who had been seen by her even though faded and not cast aside... She recognized them in the first instant and from then could not leave them, and did not until death stepped in and took a hand... She, who had said hardly a word during her life, though pursuing them all of her life, uttered more words than she had ever deemed necessary... She, who recognized those who had not been recognized by others, did not recognize her own sister at the end... So that is what I did, but how could I not do it? If you had been in my shoes would you not have done the same?'

I crept up to her. I opened the umbrella and placed it over her head. We sat huddled together under the umbrella. Grandmother stroked my hair.

'What was I expected to do?' she said. 'I thought it was the hand of God. I wanted a son so desperately, a son to carry on... then how could we face the shame of it if they ever found out whose child he was, how could we? It was better you died... wasn't it Iris... wasn't it? But I told him... I told Compton whose child he was... that's all... nothing else... at least I did that... Was it my guilt? I don't know. I told him before he left for University, but it was as if he already knew, as if he knew everything. His eyes... his eyes gave it away... he turned his back on me... How can I forget his eyes...? Like yours Iris... just like yours before you died. I was unrecognized... It was his eyes that made me tell him the little I did... turned his back and left... and through it all I neglected my daughters... became preoccupied with money and land and property and business and in the process cast people aside with indifference, allowing myself to become calloused... cast aside my own daughters, my own flesh and blood... cast you aside... for what? To what purpose? Now she's dead... I could have helped her... but you always understood, Iris... you always knew... That is why they were so afraid of you... both our mother and father... why he beat you so and why she kept on at you so.'

CHAPTER FORTY-TWO

Grandmother has started walking the streets. One day she dressed very smartly and said she was taking a walk... She borrowed my umbrella. When she did not return after it got very dark, Rose went out to look for her and found her walking the streets and brought her back. She told Rose she has to get away from them, from the ones who faded fast, that at the moment she's afraid of bumping into them, for she still isn't ready to deal with them... at least not as yet... that they are the cause of the cracks, that the sounds she keeps hearing are their voices. At least she can now recognize the sounds... that they are telling her all kinds of things, forcing her to look at things anew... that she's listening, but she can only take so much, only understand some of what they're saying, and even when she doesn't, the words are battering at her very soul, for she's an old woman, no longer the woman she used to be, so she had to get out to walk the streets, to get away until she can truly deal with it, until she can deal with the voices and not cast them aside.

Grandmother is taping the walls, the floors, the beams to keep them out, to keep the voices out.

Grandmother is removing the tapes from the wall and floors and beams so she can hear the voices.

Grandmother now calls me Iris. She holds me and says she's beginning to see things in a different light... like Gladys Davis's husband, George Davis, who it is reputed, was almost blinded by the burst of light when he first stepped off the plane on his return from England... who, it is reputed, has never fully recovered his sight because of his unnamed country's blinding light, and in the blinding it was as if he gained new sight, and in the sighting has begun to read this unamed country with its own history and its own legacies in a different light... Grandmother said I might understand, having pursued the word more than anyone else in the family. Perhaps I have come to an understanding as she is trying to do. She asked me to go with her on her walks but then she becomes very silent. We never fail to take the umbrella.

Aunt Eileen says I am not well. Granny Irma says I am not well. Whenever they speak to me they do so very gently... they lower their voices as if talking to a sick person...

The paint is peeling off of the house. The wood ants are taking over, Rose says...

CHAPTER FORTY-THREE

A letter arrived for Rose today. Her husband has found the gold he has been looking for for so long. He is coming back to town... Rose cried. She showed the letter to my grandmother. She told her she will take care of her and that there is no need for her to worry about going to a home like Ruby, or not having a roof over her head, that she, Rose Elmfield, will buy the house from her and look after her in her old age.

Granny Irma says she never thought she would live to see the day that Rose would have enough money to buy any property, much less this property. She says she never thought she would live to see the day that Rose would one day be in charge of the property and they would be beholden to her. She says her time is running out, that too many changes are taking place that she can account for.

Aunt Eileen says she will never get over the shock. That Rose came to her and said that her husband will be starting a business and he would need some help, not having the experience and education, so perhaps she would take on the job of manager of the business. That he now has the money to give her a good salary, better than she can get anywhere else. She said that she, Eileen Gomez, has come to this but in these days of uncertainty she has to swallow her pride whole and take whatever scraps she can get, and at least with the salary she would be able to rent her own place and not be beholden to anyone and can at last give her daughter a chance to leave this unnamed, godforsaken country.

CHAPTER FORTY-FOUR

Arabella... Arabella... oh Arabella, they're sending me away to America, to Granny Irma's and Grandmother's brother Percival Matthew Robertson... What a long name it is, such a long name. I don't know him... Mind you I've heard of him... He lives in Brooklyn... It's the same place where my father's brains were spattered. It's the same place where a jealous, hate-filled woman blew my father's brains out at the break of dawn, his death the final breaking point for my mother... she who felt she'd received more bad breaks than she'd bargained for... but then he lived at a break-neck speed, Aunt Eileen said, so he got what was coming to him, didn't he? Didn't he get his just deserts? she asked Granny Irma... a man who could not break away from women, who made a habit of having women until it became a habit of mind, a man too good-looking for his own good. I'll be going to Brooklyn, Arabella, a place I've only seen in the movies, to stay at the house of one Percival Matthew Robertson, my great uncle who must be as old as the hills and that's very old, Arabella. I believe you're also as old as the hills, aren't you, Arabella? Older than we can ever imagine, as old as El Dorado... El Dorado, where I've finally decided you really came from. You didn't just come from anywhere, Arabella, not you. Oh no, you're too special for that... Oh yes you are... You came from El Dorado, that faraway, ancient place one only dreams about. You do know about El Dorado, don't you, Arabella? Of course you do. As quiet as you are I've never taken you for granted... no, no... But don't be afraid for me... I can see it in your eyes... You see my great uncle's children say they'll take care of me. They told granny Irma they'll look after me as if I were there very own. He has three children Granny Irma says... two daughters and a son. I don't know their names but I'll eventually find out. I wonder what I'll call him, Arabella? Will I say, 'Hello, great-uncle. I'm Margaret... the one who's not well... the one who has been acting strangely'? Or should I say, 'Hello, Mr. Robertson. I'm Margaret, the strange one... the one sent to you'? Or maybe, 'It's a pleasure to meet you, Percival. You've been most kind to have me... the lost one... You see, it's said that I can't find myself and because of this I haven't been myself. I hope you'll excuse me, but you see I lost my mother and in losing her I began to lose myself'? How does that sound, Arabella? Do you like the sound of it? Who knows? Anyway, whatever, Aunt Eileen and Granny Irma called him on the phone last night and spoke with him. I heard them telling him I'm not well and they know this is sudden but something has to be done. Guy will be leaving for University so he will accompany me.

They think it's best I go away for a while, that I'm acting as strangely as my grandmother, that we are two of a kind but whereas she is old, I can still be helped; that I am not myself, have not been myself for a long time; that something is obviously wrong and perhaps America would be the best place. So I thought about it and I thought about you, Arabella, and I thought how you came here without any choice, the same way I am being sent without any choice... You came here from a place called El Dorado that I've only seen in my dreams, but perhaps I'll meet someone in America who'll talk to me the same way I've talked to you. Who knows? Someone to help me come to some kind of understanding... not a whole lot... just some kind... and when I do I'll return one day as you're going to return to El Dorado. You would like to go back to that faraway, ancient place called El Dorado, wouldn't you, Arabella, where all the bright-winged parrots and macaws, looking just like you, dwell with the same charcoal rings around their eyes, just like yours... Oh one day I'll return, I'll return... dressed-up in all my finery...

When I first opened up the cage and called to her... *Arabella... Arabella...* very gently... she didn't seem to understand, but then I reminded her that she was the one who asked me to send her back to El Dorado and I was just following her wishes. I heard her ask me. I'm sure if anyone had been around they'd agree with me. First she asked me, then she said 'El Dorado. It's time for me to return, Margaret,' very distinctly. I heard her, I tell you I heard her... she even called my name. That's why I said to her, 'You've gone with me various places, we played together, but then your wings were clipped, but you can fly now... Come.' At first she just looked at me, at first she seemed to hesitate, as if afraid... So I said again to her, 'Come', and it was only then she put out her bird's foot very tentatively and perched on my hand. I took her out. At first I could see she still thought her wings were clipped for she did nothing, she just remained perched on my hand, then all of a sudden she stretched out her wings and I could see how surprised she was, as if a new kind of feeling soared through her body. I placed my ear against her bird's heart and it was drumming ever so fast. It made a deep throbbing sound as if her bird's chest was the skin of a drum. She stretched out her wings again and again, then she paused... trembled... then she gave a loud shriek... It rang out in the quiet neighbourhood, sending out echoes like bells, as if she were a bell-bird, her bell-sounds making the quiet neighbourhood throb, making the neighbourhood come alive, making it one big drum, making it her sounding board... It was like no sound I'd ever heard and I liked the sound of it. I could hear Rose and Granny Irma calling out, but then I heard

Grandmother. She kept shouting, 'That's it... that's the sound I've been hearing... Sounds to me like something's cracking... Get it, get the piece of crochet, Rose, Rose. Quick, I think I've caught it... that's it, that's the sound... Sounds to me like a sea of voices. Do you hear it... the voices... like bells?' Then Grandmother called out in return to Arabella... loud and clear... and it was if Grandmother was responding to the drumming sounds, as if she could understand the message of the drum on Arabella's bird-chest, throbbing like the skin of a drum, as if fingers were inside of her bird-body beating out the sounds. Arabella called back to Grandmother... they sounded so alike you couldn't tell the difference, but then they hushed her up, they held my grandmother down on the bed and hushed her up. They slapped her across the mouth because she was acting hysterical, Aunt Eileen said, and only a slap can help hysterics... For, Aunt Eileen said, the way Grandmother sounded, she didn't like the sound of it at all... not at all...

It was then Arabella revealed her plume of glittering colours. She burst into flames. For the first time since I knew her she revealed her true colours... burnt gold... rose petal... vermillion... royal charcoal... glowing charcoal shaped like a ring around her eyes. Oh, I wish you could see her... she is so impressive. I hope it doesn't go to her head this time... But it's as if she's afraid to move, as if she's come to a standstill, as if she's bedazzled by her own colours, struck by her own beauty. And so I struck her like I struck my own mother because I'd wanted her to live, I'd wanted her to burn bright. I struck Arabella. Burn bright, I said to her, burn bright like you've never burned before and in the burning you'll bring her back to life won't you? You'll make my mother live, won't you? It was only then she made a slight movement and turned her charcoal-ringed eyes to me. She turned around and in the turning, for a moment, it was just as if my mother's charcoal arm encircled me, and in the encircling consoled me. Arabella's charcoal-ringed eyes seemed to glow, so I whispered again, Burn bright... burn bright, Arabella, like you've never burned before. She spun around and lifted her wings. Her feathers rippled over my face as if she were caressing it. She tried to pull herself away, she lurched forward, and for a moment I thought her wings had been clipped for too long, she had been caged for too long, she no longer remembered how to fly. But then she steadied herself and slowly lifted her wings once again and in the lifting rose up... up... into the air, a wheel of colours bedazzling the eyes, making me lurch, a wheel of colours spinning round and round, wheeling round and round and round... her charcoal-ringed eyes now lit up... alight... She is soaring up to the casuarina tree. She has stopped there for a while as if getting her bearings. Now she's coming back, she's come right back and perched onto my shoulder. She is rubbing her beak against my cheek. How she preens and sparkles in all her glory. Oh, she has added so many colours to my life, she has added so many new sounds to my life, sounding me out. You should see her, with her wings flared, a skirt of feathers flowing round about her, all in a swirl, leaving me in a swirl. Now she's soaring up again in her strike for freedom, in her strike to return to El Dorado, a faraway, ancient place as old as the hills, as old as Arabella, where other bright winged parrots and macaws with charcoal rings around their eyes also dwell. Up... and up... and up... over Mr. Wood's house... over the casuarina trees... up... and up... and up... on the wing... on the swing... on the wheel... wheeling round... and round and round... Oh you should see her... she's a sight for sore eyes...

'The bird has flown. Someone opened the bird's cage and let the macaw out. Where is Margaret? Where's that child? How did that bird get out? How in heaven's name did that bird get out? Come back here. Come back here... Where are you going? Get back here at once... This is a madhouse... a madhouse!' Aunt Eileen shouted as she ran behind my grandmother.

Grandmother ran to the window, she ran and threw the crocheted web out as if to capture Arabella. 'She's broken out of her cage!' she shouted. 'The beautiful bird is gone... she's rainbow-coloured... Do you see her? There's Margaret... Isn't she beautiful, Margaret? She's broken out, she escaped through the cracks... she's wheeling around... full circle... she's going around in circles. Do you see her, Margaret? It has all come full circle.' Aunt Eileen and Rose grabbed at my grandmother, the three of them wheeling round and round in circles to get to grandmother's bed. 'The bird broke out, Eileen... It was so unhappy in that cage... so it broke out... it broke free, Eileen,' my grandmother said as they finally got her to her bed.

Meanwhile Granny Irma just looked on at the goings-on in sheer amazement. She kept bobbing her head back and forth as if she couldn't believe it... Her head moved like a ball hanging on a neck thread... up and down... up and down... making me quite dizzy... as if she couldn't believe her eyes. 'Look what my sister has come to,' she kept repeating, 'Look what we've all come to. Lord have mercy on us all.'

CHAPTER FORTY-FIVE

At the crack of dawn the following day I got up from my bed very quietly as I could hardly sleep thinking of all that had been going on, thinking of Arabella's flight and how much I would miss her, thinking how Arabella's charcoal-ringed eyes reminded me of my mother's charcoal arm encircling me, holding me. So I got up very quietly from my bed and went to Grandmother's room. She was sitting up in bed as if she'd also had a restless night. She looked as if she were in a deep muse. She didn't seem surprised when I lay down next to her. She didn't say anything, instead she sat very still with her head on her shoulder as if she were listening. It was only then I realised how thin she'd become... Her bones protruded... she'd shrunk... she was so thin. She smiled at me, a bare crack of a smile, like an opening, as if she wanted to open up. And so I opened up to her and began to tell her about me, Margaret Saunders, being an eavesdropper... the way I used to go around trying to pick up the crumbs of their conversations. I told her about Arabella. I told her how dumbstruck Arabella had been after she was sent here without choice to this house. How she'd come from El Dorado, the place one only dreams about. I told her about the wheel of colours which she'd also seen the day Arabella broke out and made a strike for her freedom. I told her how I struck Arabella and in the striking Arabella burned bright, and uttered sounds never heard before by me. I told her about my mother, her daughter, and how much I'd wanted her to live and in the wanting I struck Arabella, and in the striking it was as if I struck a match because she seemed to spurt into a flame of colours and her bird's heart beat like a drum, drumming out all other sounds. My grandmother was listening. She didn't laugh out loud and say what nonsense are you talking, Margaret... Your head is full of nonsense. No, my grandmother didn't laugh as if I were some kind of joke. She listened, taking it all in, letting what I had to say sink in. She didn't chase me away, she really listened and when I was finished she asked me to tell her again about opening Arabella's cage and freeing Arabella, making her a wheel of colours, allowing her to return to El Dorado. She called Arabella the bird of time... Well, I told her again. She smiled... a crack of a smile broke across her face lighting up her burnt-wood flesh. She gave a small laugh... crackled laughter... her voice crackled as she said to me, 'I've learned so much... so much... as if... as if... I've taken a leap in the dark... as if... as if... I've grown by leaps and bounds... no longer bound... The voices... I can hear the voices... as if I'm linked to the voices... the way I felt linked to the voice of the bird of time...' Then she cradled my head on her chest of bone and held me against her as if I were her child, as if I were her daughter. I could hear the drumming sound beating against her bone-chest.

CHAPTER FORTY-SIX

It was not until just before I left for the United States with my brother Guy, to stay with my great-uncle, that grandmother was able to get a chance to speak to me again, as people were coming in and out of the house. There was a constant flow of people moving in and out after the news of my grandmother, Kathleen Harriot, began to spread like wildfire, seeing how small this unnamed country is. Flame-coloured tongues fanned rumours of Kathleen Harriot gone mad ... Oh yes, rumours fanned by word-throwers were already spreading like wildfire about Kathleen Harriot going mad, if not already gone, at the thought of her house cracking up right before her eyes. Rumours were spreading about the winds of change that must be taking place in our unnamed country after hearing of the change in Kathleen Harriot. Rumours were spreading like wildfire about Kathleen Harriot hearing voices that were telling her all sorts of things about her family long dead, even the ones who had faded fast with no record of burial, voices which were recalling the spirit of her long-dead sister Iris who'd never left this house until death stepped in and took a hand, voices which were making Kathleen Harriot reclaim her history, strange voices telling her of her country's legacies, of the history of this unnamed country, admonishing voices, voices recalling a time when our great great great great grandparents were ambushed and violently shackled and collared and dumped together like heaps of blind coal, all chain-bound, all slave-bound, but some also fear-bound, hate-bound, suicide-bound, slaughter-bound, sullen-bound, survive-at-all-costs-bound, blank-look-bound, blank-out-bound, despair-bound, amnesia-bound, tractable-bound, black-out-bound, run-amok-bound, word-bound, hope-bound, maroon-bound, spirit-bound, god-bound, but all chain- bound, all slave-bound, bound to the point of no return on ships steered by men who lacked colour and by that very lack were given the means to be members of the human race while they, because of their stained skins, were made more visible and so sold and designated as human beasts of burden at a place no one could ever put a name to.

In the midst of the rumour spreading, when verbal exchanges were become more heated and passions inflamed over what had actually taken place in Kathleen Harriot's house bequeathed to her by her great great grandparents, who had faded fast with no record of burial, with the temperature already at extraordinarily high levels, forcing people to keep their doors and windows open just to get a breath of fresh air, in the midst of the heat of the moment, doors slammed in our house... bang bang... like gun shots. Voices exclaimed... ooooooooh... Voices prayed... Dear Lord, come to our aid in this time of trial, in this time of uncertainty. Feet stamped... bup bup bup... Strangers, never before seen, sank onto our worn-out chairs and begged for glasses of water just to cool their inflamed-bodies. Aunt Eileen hid her face in shame, as she called it, pure shame at what she considered herself exposed to, so it was not until the day of my fifteenth birthday my grandmother finally had a chance to really speak to me. She spoke to me all in a tremor as if... as if I mattered, as if I were truly her daughter, her eyes so bright with tears they shimmered, and in a flash I remembered Arabella as she took wing and rose up... up... into the air... a ripple of winged feathers which seemed to change from moment to moment as if by magic... all because of grandmother's tears. I remembered Arabella's fluid wings... on the wing... burnt-gold... rose petal... vermillion... royal blue... glowing charcoal that ringed her eyes, so much like my mother's charcoal arm as she clutched it against her lopsided chest when I returned home from Rose's father's house in the country. And I remembered how I struck my mother's face, struck and struck to make her burn bright again, to elicit fire when she stopped breathing, after she came to a complete standstill, death-stricken, ashen-faced. I couldn't believe she'd died. I wanted her to live, to burn bright again, so I told myself that she was alive, my mother was alive, so I struck-out and struck her ashen-face... and charcoal-ringed-eyed Arabella dressed-up in all her glowing finery struck out of her cage and diving into the air rose up and vanished into some faraway place called El Dorado that I've only dreamed about, ancient El Dorado where bright-winged parrots and macaws with the same charcoal rings around their eyes dwell... And this time she didn't go beyond herself, this time it didn't go to her head.

My grandmother spoke to me, really spoke to me as if I were her daughter, but she also spoke to me along with Gladys Davis and her husband George Davis, who, when he returned from England, it is said, almost went blind because he found the light of this unnamed country of his birth too harsh for him... Apparently Gladys Davis had been speaking with her husband all along, telling him all the stories about my grandmother Kathleen Harriot, and what had been going on from the time the first crack appeared, telling him about the house of secrets and the crocheted web and the cracks and ambushed souls and voices that ambushed the unwary whether by night or day, about the rumours and legends that were already building-up around my grandmother, seeing how small this country is... So with all the snooping and hunting I've been doing, feeding on the crumbs of their conversations and secrets, I just didn't realize that all along Gladys Davis was passing-on all that information to her husband. I never even suspected, with all the hunting and snooping I've been doing, I never even suspected, never ever imagined I'd have to take him into account. If only Arabella were here I would have so much to tell her, especially after speaking with Grandmother who has changed so much, who seems so much wiser to me, though not to Aunt Eileen. Aunt Eileen thinks Grandmother is crazy, that those voices she keeps talking about mean she's gone crazy. To call out to a bird was crazy, she said, to call an ordinary macaw the bird of time, she exclaimed, was beyond her... What bird of time she asked Granny Irma? She's no different to Margaret she said, head full of mad ideas and dreams... But to me, grandmother seems wiser, as if she knows so much more... for didn't she say in front of Gladys and George Davis that we're all voices linked together, linked together in an unnamed muse... Yes, I do know a little more since Arabella struck-out and vanished into that distant ancient place called El Dorado that I've only dreamed about and where I now know Arabella came from, and also since my talk with my grandmother and Gladys and George Davis... for didn't George Davis say that we speak to each other across chasms of time. Grandmother looked up at him as if struck by his words, for she kept repeating, yes, yes, that's it, George. He said it was as if he were now seeing things afresh, now reading his unnamed country's legacies in a different way, a different light, which he feels he started doing from the time he returned from England, when as soon as he stepped off the plane he found the burst of light too much for him and so for months he walked around just as if he were blind or drunk, which at the beginning had terrified him, though he'd never said it to anyone since he couldn't explain it at the time... his sight sundered by the burst of light... But after he began to hear from his wife of what had been taking place... and of Arabella's flight... for him it all symbolised a breakthrough from the ambush of colonial history... It made him begin to see his unnamed country's legacies in a new, liberating, terryifying, sobering light... How else could he explain it, he asked... He, George Davis, who as his wife could confirm, had never been one for any kind of book learning, a simple man... Oh if only Arabella were here I'd have so much to tell her. She'd find it as hard to believe as I find it, to hear them talking the way they did, in a different way and including me, not excluding me from their conversations.

My grandmother then spoke, so quietly, that we had to lean forward until our hands actually touched so as to hear her. 'We inhabit a strange web of fictions replete with family histories rooted in violence... rage... incest... sorrow... betrayals... I know it... we know it, don't we? And yet, and yet there is something marvellous in us that can change, can make us turn the bleak messages of the past into a rich foundation of truth... and... and... maturity.' That's what my grandmother said, and I could hardly believe it for she was speaking in such a wise way, like an old woman of wisdom, like one of those old wise woman who retain all the world's secrets. She spoke as if she was groping for words to get to some kind of understanding... groping once again in the dark... but in a different way... a night-stalker turned word-stalker turned quest-stalker, and this time coming up with something real, as if, in her own mind, finally she was getting to the source of the cracks... And I could hardly believe I was included in their conversations. It was an eye-opener for me, I can tell you, not leaving me out, not leaving me to pick up only the crumbs in whatever way I could, but instead talking with me to make me understand that even though my family history, my unnamed country's history, may be rooted in so much pain, suffering, violence, yet, yet, as my grandmother said, we have something within us that can change the pain and violence and suffering into something rich, glorious... and what she said brought to mind Arabella's eye-stunning colours that had left me bedazzled... Oh how surprised Adrienne and Guy and Norma and Granny Irma and Aunt Eileen would be if they had heard us that day, and if they heard what was was being said. 'Yes,' grandmother continued, sounding not in the least afraid or ashamed, 'Yes, I am not ashamed to confess that Compton whom I cherished... cherished... had been an incestuous child... the child of my sister... Iris... and my brother... Stan.' She then turned to me and laid her hands on me as if she were blessing me... just like the priest does... At first I was very surprised, but then it all seemed to fit in with the day and the conversation and all that had been taking place... My grandmother turned to me and said with just a crack of a smile, 'You, Margaret, will go with my blessing... You may not understand everything I have to say, for after all it's only now at my old age I have come to such an understanding... only after the cracks and voices that ambushed me, the unwary one... voices that ambushed my very soul. It's only now I've come to a partial understanding... but one day you will, I'm sure you eventually will... Compton was a son I idolised... you, Margaret, you are a daughter... The wheel... for that is what it was... the terrifying wheel that broke into and cracked the walls of my house has come full circle... wheel and wing... All your conversations, Margaret, with Arabella, which I now call the bird of time and which you told me about, may yet free you from bondage to the terrors of the witch-craft of the past... I feel like an old witch, George... Gladys... like an old witch exorcising the witch-craft of the past... me, Kathleen Harriot, an old witch...' She laughed and they laughed and I laughed.

She continued, 'It's amazing how houses are sometimes self-made prisons, unhappy cages in which it becomes easy to confine ourselves... amazing isn't it? But when the web breaks nothing is too trivial is it, eh? Nothing. Or too terrible for that matter... to be discarded... without plumbing... without going very deeply into the mystery of self-knowledge... isn't that so? George? Gladys? Or am I mad as they all seem to think, except for Margaret? Except for her, they think I'm mad, your old friend talking like this. Isn't it amazing? Don't you think so, Margaret? Your grandmother of all people... but what I say matters, because it's there begins a fiery baptism that brings a name to the land of our birth, and that name is written in our hearts.'